BEAUTY
REBORN

ELIZABETH LOWHAM

Visit us at shadowmountain.com

Library of Congress Cataloging-in-Publication Data
CIP on file
ISBN 978-1-63993-106-4

Printed in the United States of America
Lake Book Manufacturing, LLC, Melrose Park, IL

10 9 8 7 6 5 4 3 2 1

To Brady,

who supports me in every book,

in every thing, *even the whimsy,*

always and forever.

PROLOGUE

It's true what the folktale says: I did choose to live with the beast. But not for the reason you think. Not to save my father. Not even to save myself.

In truth, I was hoping I'd be eaten.

Everything began with Stephan Galliford, who had a gleam in his gaze from the first moment he saw me, who bent low and kissed my hand and lingered.

Stephan asked me three times to marry him. Three times, I said no.

After that, he didn't ask.

When the news came that Father was bankrupt and we had to sell all we possessed to pay our debts, my eldest sister, Astra, wailed in such a way it might have been the death of everyone she loved—if she loved anyone besides herself, that is. Callista and Rob were more reserved in their responses, though they also grieved the loss of the home and life they'd known. Father was silently broken, the echo of a man who went through every required motion though he no longer lifted his eyes from the ground.

I alone was ungrieved. Astra hated me the more for it, but

Callista said, "It's wonderful, Beauty, that even in all this darkness, you can still find hope."

It was not hope; it was escape, albeit temporarily. But I did not correct her.

While Astra wept over the loss of every embroidered gown and jeweled brooch, I assisted Father with the auction. I smiled at potential buyers and urgently chattered about why this painting was a necessity for a regal sitting room or how that riding habit was in most excellent fashion and taste. As a lady of society had once told me, chatter was my only true skill, and I employed it relentlessly while Father did all he could to recoup the debt incurred by the loss of his silk and his ships.

Only one item at the auction gave me pause. I cradled it gently, ran my thumb along the curve of the base. I would have plucked one of the strings if not for my father's glance just then. In his eyes, I saw the longing to allow me one relic, one testament to all that was gone. But relics could not be afforded—not when I'd already seen Astra tuck a necklace away—and my violin would sell for more than my wardrobe, so it was the only contribution I could make.

Catching the attention of a lady I recognized, I said, "You've wanted your daughter to engage in a fine hobby. There is nothing so fine as music."

And the deed was done. She lifted the instrument out of my hands, leaving my fingers cold and exposed. I curled them into my palms, hugged my arms to my body, and resumed my chattering with more devotion than ever until the day was worn out, the auction done, and our once-warm house empty of soul.

When I chattered in the same way during dinner that evening, Astra screamed at me to be silent. If not for Rob's quick hand of restraint, she would have doused me with the wine from her cup.

Father scolded her sharply. "Without Beauty, I'd have accomplished little these past days. What have your tears accomplished, Astra?"

There was silence after that.

I had managed to restrain my flinch, but still I trembled. Even though I had no desire to be alone, I excused myself before they could notice my weakness.

Stephan did not come to the auction. I imagined the lord baron had not wanted his nephew and heir near a penniless, ruined girl, no matter how Stephan argued. The daughter of a wealthy merchant was one thing, but no future baron could leash himself to a peasant who would soon have to dig her fingernails in the dirt and grow calluses to survive.

I prayed for a thousand calluses and twice that many nights without a glimpse of Stephan's gleaming eyes.

But I could not pray away the haunting memory.

My father's connection to another merchant secured us a new house on the far west side of town. It was barely a hut and so close to the wild forest's border that no one had been able to use it. The land was untamable for trees, but tame it we would have to.

"Easy to make a choice when there's only one option on the table," I joked. "Perhaps we shall be fortunate enough to be offered a *second* rickety hut, this one near a wicked fairy's tower. Then our heads would truly spin."

Rob put a gentle hand on my shoulder, as he had done several times since the bankruptcy, his voice growing wearier with each reminder. "Now is not the time for jest."

But now more than ever, I could not bridle my tongue—not even when I noticed Rob swipe at his eyes while loading our few belongings into a battered wagon. My older brother cried over nothing except severe injury, and I knew it was not the loss of the house that upset him, nor even the loss of Orpheus, his purebred riding stallion. His tears were for Eva, who would not be permitted to wed a man with no fortune and no inheritance.

I opened my mouth to offer comfort, but my tongue offered only amusement, until at last, Rob sent me to find Callista, even though he had no use of her and she stood plainly with Astra.

I'm sorry, I meant to say, yet apologies remained as unavailable to my tongue as comfort. If I began apologizing, I would never stop, because there was a fire inside me, scorching my stomach, blistering my heart, and it couldn't be smothered by even a thousand regrets; it would only turn the words to fuel and burn my lungs to smoke until I could never breathe again.

So I laughed about rickety huts, even while the fire and I watched each other through narrowed eyes. I held it down through sheer force, locked beneath a tightened throat. Though the bile of my stomach boiled, none of it emerged past my teeth. Meanwhile, the chasm between me and my family that had started with my ridiculous name and grown with my ridiculous ideas only widened by the day.

As it turned out, I had been unkind to call our new home

a rickety hut. It was more a cramped cottage—small, certainly, but more stable on its foundations than I was on mine.

"*One* room?" Astra cried. "For three grown girls?"

"We're fortunate," Father said, though there was no heart in his words. "One room for Rob and me. One for you girls. It might have been all of us together."

Rob finished his circuit of the house, and he and Father discussed the land in hushed, unhopeful tones. I rolled my sleeves back and set to cleaning the thick dust of disuse from every crevice of the cottage. Reluctantly, Callista joined me.

Astra sat outside.

When the layered grime turned the curves of my fingernails black, I smiled. "There's enough dirt in this cottage to conceal a fortune greater than what Father lost. Let us hope we find it before the mice do."

Callista said, "Always so whimsical, Beauty."

It was not a compliment. It never was.

I held my teeth tight.

The house was easy enough to get in order. The land was another matter entirely. The forest had grown wild, reaching with greedy rooted fingers through every bit of land that might have otherwise been planted. Saplings and bushes could be cleared, but the network of roots in the soil was more insidious than any growth had a right to be.

"It's an enchanted forest," Callista said, peering out of the tiny kitchen window while Father and Rob were in town trying to barter for help with the clearing. "I've heard stories."

"Like what?" I shrugged. "Men poisoned by enchanted

berries? They were simply too unintelligent to sort ivy from elder."

"Then I dare you to cut a tree!"

"I will."

But when I hefted the axe, weighty and unbalanced in my hands, she rushed to stop me. "No, Beauty, don't. I think it's truly enchanted. Mrs. Halcomb once told me all the working classes refuse to hunt in this stretch of woods, and Rob said he saw something disappear between the trees."

"A fox, probably. Or a bear." Hopefully a bear. I knew nothing of bears, but there could be no better time for an introduction.

I gripped the axe with both hands and made for the door.

When Callista protested again, Astra said, "Let her go. Beauty *accomplishes* things. Perhaps she'll clear the whole forest before Father returns."

I smiled. "Perhaps you'll water the whole land with your tears, and rather than tree roots, we'll have a backyard ocean to clear."

As the door swung closed behind me, I heard Callista assure Astra that I didn't mean it, that I only liked to debate, like my instructors had taught me. Don't listen to Beauty; she's whimsical. She chases hypotheticals. She invents things. Don't believe a word. Not a word.

My dirty fingernails nearly left curved half-moons in the hardened axe handle.

I strode directly into the forest and stood beneath its black trees. We surveyed each other, shadow recognizing shadow. The trees here grew thick and tall as giants, humped roots breaking the soil at every base, branches reaching interlocking fingers to each neighboring tree, the entire forest knitted in one quilt to filter the sun.

But there was no bear.

I pressed my hand to a tree's bark, my pointer finger sinking entirely into a rut in the wood. It could suck me in and leave no trace. Suddenly, the tree felt hot to the touch, burning with the same fire that blazed in my belly.

I yanked my hand back. Then I hefted my axe high, brought it down with the movement Rob had taught me, and sank the blade into an exposed root. Nearly half the head buried! Rob would be proud.

Freeing it again was not so easy. I had to pump the handle, twist this way and that. Once I finally leveraged it free, I stared down at the wound I'd inflicted, at the sliver of pale, vulnerable wood exposed beneath its covering shell of brown bark.

I dropped the axe and covered my mouth, biting my thumb until the pain in my knuckle was all I could feel, until its white-hot flare drowned whatever was inside me.

"I didn't mean it," I whispered, crouching to touch the root. I covered the cut with my hand, but I could still see the peek of vulnerability between my fingers. Scrambling to retrieve the axe, I used it to hack a strip of linen off the bottom of my dress, nicking my calf in the process. A single drop of blood slid down the curve of my shin bone. I ignored it. With slow movements, I wrapped the root, concealing the tree's wound carefully from edge to edge.

I was a fool. I could only imagine what my family would

say about bandaging a plant; they would certainly see it while clearing the land.

Nevertheless, I secured the makeshift bandage with a gentle knot.

When I looked up, a pair of blue fairy eyes looked back.

I started, and in that blink, she vanished, only a faint shimmer in the air to confirm her passing.

After a moment, I gathered my senses and left the forest. The walk back seemed somehow a longer trek than I remembered making initially, and when I arrived home, Father and Rob had returned. They and my sisters were gathered in the yard, staring in wonder at the soil. Help would not be needed after all, because every root, sapling, and bush had vanished, just as the fairy. The land was ready for tilling.

Astra scowled at me like I'd fed her ivy berries.

Father looked at the axe in my hands, his jaw slack. "Beauty, did you . . . ?"

"The forest is enchanted, Father. Living fairy and all." I handed the axe to Rob. "We'd best stay out of it."

They were, of course, relentless, and they weaseled the full story out of me at last. Perhaps they even believed it. At first. But as Astra pointed out, fairies were not known for kindness, so why clear the land? As Callista pointed out, I'd made no wish and therefore could have invoked no magic. As Rob pointed out, I'd chopped a tree. If there really were a fairy of the forest, I'd have been cursed with pig ears or worse on the spot.

Don't listen to Beauty; she's whimsical. Don't believe a word. Not a word.

Father's troubled frown was worst of all. True or not, my story only added more to the burden he already carried. In the end, he made the decision: No one goes in the forest.

So even though I caught another glimpse of the fairy through the trees, I made no mention of it. She could have enchanted me to float, turned my nose to a snout, attached herself to me like a growth, and I would have maintained my silence all the same.

"If only Beauty could have accomplished the planting along with the clearing," Astra said, not even throwing seeds with the rest of us. "If only her fairy would advance the crops instantly to harvest."

I smiled. "If only Astra would put her tears to use as rainwater, the crops may advance to harvest just as fast."

That's the truth of how my story began: with a secret and a smile.

And one more familiar element—

The day came too quickly when we'd exhausted what little food we'd brought, our nonexistent funds, and our meager resources, and Father announced that he would hunt in the forest alone, unaccompanied even by Rob. He did not return with meat. He returned with only one thing.

A rose.

CHAPTER 1

Perhaps I startled the beast, showing up at its gate alone and empty-handed, looking not remotely like a rose thief. In the pre-dawn gloom, the great golden gate loomed before me, covered in creeping yellow vines of the finest craftsmanship, each tendril dotted with the roses this creature apparently loved so much.

Beyond the gate was a path paved in gray stone, like a trail of fog leading through lavish gardens of every flower imaginable to spring, in varieties I'd never seen in the hothouses of the city. After the gardens came the white-stone castle, with red brick at its windows and on its turrets. Even under a dim sky, it was grand. It was gorgeous.

To die here would not be so bad.

"Hullo, Beast," I called, waving even though there was no beast to be seen and not another living soul besides. "I am Robert Acton's daughter, Beauty. He plucked a rose from your many gardens, and I am here to pay his debt."

Any social tact I'd ever possessed, drilled into me by a high-society mother and a fretting governess, I'd left behind in our city house, tucked neatly on the empty shelves of its study. I'd always harbored a reckless tongue, and on the verge of death, the careful bridle that had once harnessed it was now removed. What would a beast care if its meal came with no manners and a tendency to conversation even if no one marked her? Surely it would care less than Astra did.

The golden gates shuddered at my voice, but if they felt horror at my uninvited arrival or bold announcement, they swung open regardless, and I walked the dew-covered path to the castle entrance. Its great double doors swung open in the same way, without even a word to prompt them. I only lifted my hand, and they shied away from my touch, repulsed by the very idea. Perhaps they saw the dirt beneath my fingernails, or perhaps they saw even deeper to the filth on my soul.

"I said I'm Robert Acton's daughter," I tried again, "come in his place."

Father had been very specific that the beast had appeared from thin air. But nothing appeared in the silent entryway. A coat stand shivered at my words, as did the lit silver sconces.

I worked the thick gold ring from my finger, held it up to catch the light. "I have this."

But no one answered.

When Father had gone hunting, I'd offered to go *instead* or *with* him, though the words had been embarrassing to speak, shamefully thin and hollow with no hunting skill to give them worth. Not like Rob, who was also denied. But when Father had stumbled home pale-faced and terrified, when he'd spoken of a snarling beast and a debt to be paid, when he'd pulled a rose from his pocket with not a petal crushed because the petals were pure gold, I felt a great stone of certainty settle in my stomach. Because here was something I could do, and there was nothing empty in it except me, and even if I was being hollowed out by fire, it was roaring loud as any beast.

While Astra wailed the moon into the sky as if Father's grave had already been dug, Callista comforted her. I didn't, and with her own tears, Callista called me heartless. She had no idea. Father spoke with Rob in the back room, charged him with tending the family. Meanwhile, I snuck the enchanted ring from Father's coat, the one that was meant to whisk him back to the beast after he'd finished his goodbyes. I rotated it three times around my thumb, and then the cottage was gone.

And I stood at a palace's gold gates.

When I'd come in my father's place, I'd hoped the beast might be angry at my deception. I'd never imagined it might be silent.

Seeing no other option, I dropped the ring on a table and hesitantly wandered the castle. Perhaps I would find the beast asleep. My intellectual side could not help being curious about a magical beast, and a sleeping creature would provide me the chance for observance I couldn't obtain while I was being speedily devoured. Father had not given a full description of the creature, but I could not fault him if all he'd noticed in the moment were the gleaming fangs. And the astonishingly human voice.

At the news of a talking beast, Astra had bemoaned that our forest was undoubtedly enchanted.

In return, I had bemoaned, "If only there had been some sign."

My father's eyes were on me, and his sadness was a weight I couldn't carry. He might have apologized to me, but I couldn't let that cycle begin, and the silence bore as much chance of a reprimand as an apology, so I had to fill it first. I rushed forward with questions, and the moment passed.

The castle had no shortage of rooms.

I peeked into a grand dining hall, an even grander ballroom, several sitting rooms and parlors, and a room that seemed to be devoted purely to portraits.

"Lovely castle," I remarked quietly to no one. "The loveliest I've ever seen." I smiled at my own wit. I was the only one who ever did, but wit was all I had left.

A descending staircase led me to a dungeon, which I was rather surprised to find as grand as the rest of the castle so far, a collection of cells with enough space to hold an invading army, or so it seemed at a glance. It would have been more foreboding in darkness, but every sconce lit at my approach. Callista would have been delighted at the idea of self-lighting candles but terrified to see it in action. From the time we were still in nursery rooms, she'd collected stories of magic and enchantment from any adult willing to indulge her in the telling, yet faced with our own enchanted forest, she gave it only longing side-glances and a wide berth.

Magic was overall a wistful thing in the kingdom. Fairies had once roamed wide and cast spells as they pleased, but perhaps they'd grown bored with us or come to prefer a life of seclusion. Now the sight of a fairy was rare, and they were notoriously grouchy at being seen. Only the bravest people would hunt them in hopes of receiving a granted wish. The rest of the kingdom contented itself with old stories and the dwindling magic found in family relics—a teapot that rattled in an attempt to pour itself or a vase that, once filled, always retained a teaspoon of water.

The beast's castle had no such dwindling magic. It was all fresh and crisp and eager to serve. Even the cell door swung open at my approach.

Was I meant to spend days in captivity awaiting my sentence?

I licked my lips, glancing back up the stairs. Then I stepped into the cell. It closed after me, though I heard no click of the lock. Feeling foolish, I settled onto the straw pallet inside, back pressed to the wall. Even the cell of the beast's castle had softer, cleaner surroundings than our cottage, but I was not pleased at the improvement.

In coming to the castle, I had expected a violent encounter. Father had been so certain his sentence for taking the rose was death that I had convinced myself the castle steps would run with my blood before I even reached the door. I had not even considered other possibilities. My instructors would have been disappointed in me.

But as great as my confusion was in that moment, it only increased in the next.

A slight rustle carried in the air, familiar from many afternoons in a schoolroom. I turned this way and that, impossibly expecting to see another prisoner reading a text, but I was alone. No one could have turned a page.

Then a flutter of movement—

I looked up just as a sheet of parchment sailed between the

bars of my cell. While I held myself stiffly, it floated to my lap, gentle as a feather.

There was no writing on it, only a rough drawing. A few Ls with the feet elongated, all stacked crookedly, and an arrow beside them, parallel to the backs. I plucked at the edge of the page, rotated it on its side, but the drawing became no clearer.

"Hello?" I tilted my head, peering, but there was no one on the stairs.

Stairs.

I reexamined the stacked Ls. They could perhaps be representative of a staircase. And an arrow . . .

"Was I not meant to come down here?"

My answer was the now-expected silence. But when I climbed to my feet, the cell door swung open as readily to permit my exit as it had my entrance. My cheeks burned.

"A communication with words would be appreciated." I directed my own words at the cell door, and it swung a few inches forward and back, as if wishing it could escape but finding itself on a leash. As I walked through, I touched it briefly in reconciliation. It was unfair to blame a door for the games of its master, after all.

When I reached the landing, I found another sheet of parchment, this one with another staircase and arrow. I had seen a staircase previously but had limited myself to exploring the ground floor and below. If I was here to die, one floor was as good as another.

"See now," I said, setting the sconces all atremble once more. "My father took refuge here in a storm. Before he exited the gate, he plucked a rose without permission and was told he must repay the theft with his life. My life for his—that is my bargain. I will pay the debt, but I will not be dragged about for sport."

Dawn's light spilled through the entry windows, brighter with every moment, creeping its way forward on the marble floor the way I felt the fire creep inside me.

"If I am to be devoured," I said to a silent castle, "devour me."

At the cottage, I'd had no parchment because Father's writing desk had been sold along with all the rest. Had I been able, I would have left Father a letter. I'd composed it in my mind all the same, traced the letters, folded the parchment, and left it on the table, where it would never be read because it could not be seen. It said, *Forgive me.* A girl of so many words and yet I'd only managed two.

I wrote a letter for Stephan as well.

It said, *I would rather die.*

"*Now*, beast!" I shouted.

My voice echoed back at me from every sharp angle, and the outburst startled a rug so entirely that it yanked itself from under my feet and furled away down the hall. I stumbled, barely catching myself on the cold wall to my left. The beast was either unmoved or amused. Either way, it made no appearance.

At last, I snatched up the parchment with the scribbled drawing of stairs. Perhaps this was a hunt. Perhaps it desired to watch its prey run. Perhaps it desired to eat the juicy meal of a heart wildly pumping.

And perhaps I would let it do so, but not before stabbing it in the eye with a cheese knife.

I retrieved just such an implement from the kitchens.

Then I made my way to the staircase.

It had been my first real ball. Not technically speaking, of course. I was seventeen, but since fourteen, I had been old enough to mingle in proper company instead of staying home to tend to my studies and music practice. But this was no merchant's ball, no simple affair in the home of a neighbor. It was hosted by the lord baron himself to celebrate the official naming of his heir: Stephan Galliford.

Astra fanned herself as we watched the baron with his nephew on the dais. "I've never seen a man so handsome," she whispered, even though she'd said the same of at least five young men of society within the last month.

All men of society seemed to me as stiff planks of wood, wrapped in ribbons to pretend at texture and embroidered with all the same rigid aspirations as every other plank—wealth, prestige, respect. Not Stephan. Stephan had hair the shade of autumn walnuts, with the same waves and ridges. While every other man was a post in a fence, Stephan was the laughing creek that danced around and between them as he pleased. I saw it at a glance.

Had I said as much, my sisters would have accused me of whimsy. It was my greatest crime, announced to me by every woman of town and more loudly by the ones who had been fortunate enough to know my mother, a most levelheaded lady.

I had a head of clouds, filled with such things as eclogues and existential philosophy when it should have been filled with the grounding sand of etiquette, embroidery, and egoism.

"You *must* try to catch his eye," Callista encouraged Astra, her arm hooked through our eldest sister's, her smile enough to light the room.

"I don't know that I would suggest it," I said, pitching my voice as hushed as theirs. I leaned close. "The baron may have no children of his own, but he is still a married man. The scandal would be supreme, and should you chase her husband, the baroness may hang you with her finest embroidery thread."

Neither of my sisters smiled. In fact, Astra's scowl was quite fierce. They ignored me, and once the music began and we all shifted to the edges of the dance floor, they held their huddled, blushing conversation several feet away in order to achieve privacy. Father was engaged in conversation of his own with another merchant, and Rob, ever courteous, had already asked a young lady to dance. My brother would save at least one dance for me before the night ended; he'd promised. Until then, I was on my own, the youngest of the Acton sisters and no interest to anyone.

Or so I thought.

He approached from the other side of the room, and for a moment, I thought he would stop at Astra. She did too, smiling over a perfect curtsy, already halfway through a "My lord."

He passed without a glance.

Because his eyes were on mine.

I was too shocked to curtsy. He slipped his fingers around mine, bowed low to kiss my hand, and lingered.

"Your name, maiden?" When he looked up, a twist of walnut-curl fell across his forehead.

I could scarcely speak. "Beauty Acton, daughter of R—"

"Beauty," he breathed. "How fitting." There was a gleam in his eyes. He straightened up and offered his arm. "Dance with me, Beauty."

It wasn't a question, and there was no question of my answer.

As Stephan walked me to the dance floor, I saw Astra's face, red with fury, and Callista fluttering to calm her, a moth to the flame and just as useful. And I smiled.

CHAPTER 2

It was not a hunt. Or if it was, it was a disturbing one with an unclear destination.

On the second floor, I found a door with my name carved in scrollwork and framed by roses, as if I had always lived here and the castle had been waiting for me to realize it. I stood staring for a while, then reached up and traced my finger across the delicate wooden rose petals.

At my touch, the door swung open, revealing a large bedroom with a four-poster bed on a dais, surrounded by yellow, gauzy curtains. A large window—complete with a cushioned window seat begging to host a studiously reading occupant—cast panes of golden morning light across the lavish carpets and pale birch wardrobe. The room as a whole was sunny and lifting; it may have been taken straight from my dreams.

"I don't understand," I whispered. But no one had an answer for me.

I stepped into the room. The door had no lock, but just as I registered the thought, one appeared—not to lock me in but for me to lock others out. I slid the bolt into place and had a moment of relief before I realized that if the door moved at a thought, the lock would do the same. Nothing enchanted could be trusted. Whether it moved with a mind of its own or the mind of a master, it was all the same.

The lock disappeared.

I left the room.

For hours, I wandered the castle. At one point, a rolling cart with a silver lunch tray chased me down and aggressively waved a fork until the combination of its insistence and my extended hunger broke my resolve and I broke the crust of a pie. Perhaps the meal was poisoned. Perhaps the beast practiced human methods of death as it practiced the enforcement of human laws. Yet I finished half a meat pie with no death rattle, though the pork fat and spices were increasingly heavy on my tongue.

My stomach tilted, threatening overturn. I dropped the pie and pressed a fist to my mouth until the nausea passed. The teapot rocked back and forth like an anxious governess, and the teacup butted twice against my free hand, ignoring my swat to keep it away. On its third approach, I struck back with more force than intended, shattering the little porcelain cup against the leg of the cart.

I stared at the collection of shards, but they only trembled a moment before knitting themselves seamlessly back together. The teacup settled on the tray.

Seeing the cup whole again was worse than seeing it broken.

In one swift movement, I overturned the whole tray. The shattering might have woken a village, yet every fragment and spill swept itself up and wrung itself out until lunch was replaced in full splendor. Even my pie was whole once more, without a bite taken.

It was a farce. The whole castle. In nature, there was always a scar to betray the shattered, and that was if they managed to heal at all.

"Enough games, beast," I said, breathing heavy. "Either administer your punishment or see me leave."

I stood still for several minutes. Then, leaving the cheese knife on the tray, I walked down two flights of stairs and out the front door.

The afternoon sunlight slanted into my eyes, dazzling. I took a moment to adjust, eyes shaded, blinking down at the gray stone path. I debated plucking my own rose; that would certainly earn me a response. But then there would be two debts, and I could pay only one.

I made for the gate. It shuddered at my approach. Just as I lifted a hand—

"Don't go."

I whirled around.

But no one was there. Only a sea of flowers, trembling in the breeze. Only a towering white castle, sunlight glazing the windows.

It had been a soft voice. Perhaps even . . .

Broken.

I turned back to the gate, stared out at the forest beyond. The shadows were long and oppressive. I looked at the shining castle.

And I stayed.

I couldn't bear the silence. It was the worst part of that big, echoey castle. There was plenty of movement as enchantments ran with and without my interference, but it was all silent—the candles lit silently, the brooms swept silently, the tea poured silently and without a drop of spill. If I strained my ears, the most I got for my trouble was a whisper of sound like a light breeze through leafless trees.

I had never lived in a silent home before. Though I was the worst culprit of noise, I was never the only one. Between Astra's boisterous laughter, Callista's talent for song, and Rob's clumsiness in small spaces, there was always chatter and clatter, be it our home in the city or our new cottage.

Now I was alone in an empty castle, and my bootheels on the marble staircase bellowed like a mountain goat in all the silence. Even if I held my tongue, I was the loudest thing this castle hosted. Perhaps that was why I mortified it so.

The rolling tray brought meals to my room whenever I hungered, and for the two days following my arrival, I saw and heard no other sign of the beast. On the third day, I thought of quill and parchment, and they were mine, along with a writing desk that somehow fit itself along the wall without shrinking the room's space.

What do you want with me? I wrote. I lifted my paper in the air and released it. It fluttered away gently, slipping beneath my door with all the silence of any other enchantment.

The beast sent no response, not even another rough drawing, and the longer I studied the first two, which I'd gathered into my room, the more I became convinced he couldn't hold a quill, much less write. The strokes were too wide for any quill I'd seen and smudged at every edge. Perhaps he'd scribbled it with a claw dipped in ink.

He could certainly speak. Yet he chose not to.

On the third day, a bar of soap began to hover obnoxiously about me like a massive fly. Though I was due for a bath—my filth must have mortified the pristine castle as much as my noise—I was not about to disrobe in a stranger's house.

The soap drove me from my room, but no matter where I wandered, I could not find a room which might belong to the beast. There were many bedrooms, of course, all grand, with tapestries of great hunts and conquering kings. One had a purple rug, the likes of which might have purchased my father's entire lost fortune twenty times over. But none had personalization. If the beast occupied a room, he did so without disturbing it and without so much as a trinket or a door plaque to mark it his. What a lonely idea.

At last, I stopped to rest in a ballroom. I lay on the polished hardwood and studied the chandelier above, attempting to count the candles but losing track each time. Did palaces such as this exist without enchantments? Did they contain a thousand servants to light a thousand candles? I hummed the old melody of an early music lesson as my mind wandered.

Without warning, a harpsichord in the corner struck up the same relaxing tune.

I bolted to my feet, nearly tripping over myself, though my heart calmed when I realized no one sat at the keys. The music reverberated from every wall, breaking the silence like an energetic morning rooster. Despite myself, I smiled, then laughed in delight.

I took a step and turned on my toes. With what seemed to be delight of its own, the instrument switched to an upbeat country jig. I had no partner, but I danced all the same, and as I held half an arch for my imaginary peers to duck beneath, I joined my voice to the harp-hearted keys:

"Lolly Lyla at the door / Wonder who she's looking for"—the harpsichord interjected a trill of arpeggios—"Dance, my darling, all the day / Her poor boy has gone away."

Between the dancing and the singing, I quickly lost my breath. Though I loved music, I was no singer, not like Callista. When we lived in the city, it would have been Astra at the harpsichord with Callista's angelic voice carrying the melody to the heavens. As for me, my only musical talent—

A violin appeared on the harpsichord bench, polished wood shining in the light.

I came to an abrupt stop, panting for breath. When the instrument didn't vanish, I hesitantly approached, then lifted it by the neck. A bow appeared in my hand.

The harpsichord, which had fallen silent, plucked a few quiet keys.

As I settled both violin and bow into place, my eyes stung. My violin in the city had been a fine instrument, but it paled next to the sleek work of art in my hands, and when I drew the bow across the strings, the violin sang with a voice to rival Callista. The ballroom windows burst open, sunlight streaming in to cast patterned reflections on every wall.

Once I started, I couldn't stop. My favorite sonata first.

Then every piece I'd ever poured hours into, every melody my mind could recall or invent, running one over the other like a river on its way to the falls. All the while, the harpsichord never wavered in its accompaniment, complementing my performance as if it could read my mind to anticipate the notes. Even if I warbled an intonation, it struck the closest harmony possible, covering my mistakes with its enchanted elegance.

I played until my arms ached.

When I was finally satisfied enough to lower the violin, sweating with exertion and grinning at the empty harpsichord as its final note faded in the air, the castle seemed at least tolerable.

Now I had a way to fill the silence.

I refused to set the violin down, afraid it would vanish if I did. Surely another one would appear with a thought, but I had the selfish impulse that another one wouldn't do. It must be *this* one. There was no need to tune it—it was always in tune, and if I tried to adjust the strings at all, it would only right itself. In the same way, the bow never needed rosin, and though I played relentlessly, I never broke a hair.

At the end of the day, I carried it to my room and tucked it carefully into the hollow beneath my window seat.

The pesky bar of soap returned, flitting around my head. It brought a bathtub with it this time, gleaming silver before the fireplace as a cheerful, low fire crackled to life. The water in the tub steamed gently. Even from the other side of the room, I could smell rose blossoms, my mother's favorite bath scent.

I glanced at the door. In three days, I had not been disturbed.

I could not remain unbathed forever.

Would I be here forever?

Setting my jaw, I crossed the room and bolted the door. A second bolt appeared, and I slid that one in as well. I undressed before I could change my mind and slipped into the blissfully hot water.

For a few moments, it was heaven, but then it grew harder to breathe as I imagined at any moment the door might rattle. I scrubbed as quickly as I could, outpacing the enchanted soaps and brushes that flitted around me. At least the towel was quick, as if sensing my unease.

I reached for my dress before I'd even finished drying. But I had been right to worry.

It was gone.

"Give me my clothes back," I snapped. My heart began to pound. "Now."

The wardrobe snapped open, proudly displaying a velvet gown of gleaming amber with lace at the collar and gems in the bodice.

"No, *mine*." My voice turned shrill. "Right now. Give me my clothes back. Give them to me now!"

The wardrobe shuddered and withdrew the dress, closing its doors. It seemed to droop, but my plain linen clothes appeared folded on the chair where they had been before. They were spotlessly clean.

I yanked on my shift and dress, glancing at the door. Only once I was fully clothed could I breathe again.

A floating brush attempted to strike at my wet hair, but I

pushed it away, and it relented, as the wardrobe had. I shivered and wrapped my arms around myself.

Had the magic forced itself on me, I would have had no way to fight it.

The thought was enough to drive me from my room and out the front doors of the castle. Night had fallen, but despite my shivers, I sat on a stone bench in the garden and refused to move. In the woods far beyond the castle, something howled.

So there were beasts in the forest after all.

Once the land around the cottage had been cleared of growth, there had been a sense of elation around the cottage. Father and Rob had tilled immediately, borrowing what they needed from neighbors, and all of us but Astra had assisted with planting. It was then our elation fell—because it was then we realized the true struggle of living off the land. We could plant, but we could not grow. Only the seasons could. And while the seasons took time to work, we still needed food.

Father and Rob searched for trade work. Callista was able to hire out embroidering a gown here and there for old friends in town. Astra would have been the better choice—her embroidery would befit a queen—but she would rather starve than face the humiliation of serving those who had once been peers. I tried to offer my own services, but my talents were in reading and writing, luxuries unaffordable to our neighbors. Anyone who could afford such a tutor for their children would hire a real scholar, not a peasant girl.

It weighed heavily on Father—having so many mouths to feed and only a few capable of work. I wanted to tear Astra's hair out for her pride, but it would have only added to Father's burden, so with burning cheeks, I asked Callista if she could teach me to improve my own needlework. She tried, and I tried, but a future where I could practice enough to be of use was far distant. The crops would provide for us before I could.

I worked late one night by the fire, squinting to see my stitches by the flickering light. Father came and leaned on the worn mantel above me.

"I should have made arrangements with Stephan," he said quietly. "It was clear he fancied you, and if I hadn't waited, you might be happily married and safe from this ruin."

I pricked my thumb.

After sucking the wound, I choked out, "He asked me to marry him, Papa. I said no."

"Oh." Father's eyes studied me, too bright in the firelight, and I prayed they couldn't read anything they might find. "I wasn't aware."

Astra was in the kitchen, and she heard. She held her tongue for three days, until one evening we carried firewood in together, and she looked down at her raw hands, at a splinter that had sunk into what had once been her nimble thumb, used for delicate stitches and lifting porcelain teacups, not for doing the work of a man at the remote edge of a forest, so far removed from the idea of high society it may as well have been a place in the sky. Then she looked at me and said coldly, "You didn't deserve him."

We both knew who and what she meant.

He should have asked me, her eyes said. *I would have said yes.*

I had no doubt she would have. In that moment, the frozen shell of my heart thought they made a perfect pair indeed.

At least now there was one less mouth to feed at the cottage. I sighed, trying to pull my collar higher to ward off the chill from my wet hair. I breathed into my hands and pressed my slightly warmed palms to my cold ears. The castle loomed at my back, casting dim light from its windows, but not quite enough to reach the bench where I'd retreated.

"Don't turn around," said a voice behind me.

I stiffened, barely registering the request in time to obey. I trembled with more than the cold.

"Why?" I rasped.

The answer I received was a sheet of parchment floating onto my lap. It was the letter I'd written, though it could hardly be called that.

"What does it say?" His voice was still surprising in its softness, as it had been at the gate, but upon a second listen, I heard the thinnest edge of a growl.

I ached to turn, but I held myself stiff.

"It asks what you want with me," I said.

There was a long pause. He'd come silently; perhaps he had left the same way. Perhaps I was alone again. I tried to hold my posture, but my mind became more and more convinced that at any moment, he would seize me from behind.

I leapt to my feet and whirled, gasping for breath.

But he was gone, as was the parchment.

CHAPTER 3

The beast could not read. I don't know why the realization surprised me. Perhaps because if a beast could speak, I imagined he could do anything.

I had adopted Father's term for him, "beast," but what did it mean, really? His rumbling voice had certainly been human enough, even if it snarled like a wolf at the edges.

When I could no longer abide the cold of the garden and finally returned to my room, I found a book of loose sheet music waiting outside my door. I hesitated, looking around, trying to determine if the beast had left it for me or if it had been a gesture by the castle itself. In the end, I cleared my throat and whispered "Thank you" before gathering the music and slipping into my room. I serenaded the moon with the violin until I was too tired to lift the bow, and then I curled around the instrument and fell asleep in my window seat.

The next day, I took my violin—*my* violin, how presumptuous of me—back to the ballroom for the harpsichord's accompaniment. I practiced the two new pieces I'd learned the previous evening, playing through each until I could read without faltering, even if not with perfection. It was perhaps unwise to have accompaniment before I mastered my own playing, but the harpsichord felt almost like company, and I was helpless to resist.

By the time the lunch hour arrived, I'd given myself a thorough headache by concentration and unrelenting sound, but I smiled all the same, and it was not the stiff smile that held something behind my teeth.

This was not what I had imagined coming to the castle would hold.

After I finished lunch in my room, I sat at the writing desk and penned a new "letter." This one said, *My name is Beauty.* Once it had fluttered off, I sat on the staircase outside my room, picking at the cold, smooth marble of the stairs. Thin veins of gold traced through the white stone, like tiny rivulets of water forging paths in a white beach. I'd never seen a white beach, but I thought they were the most beautiful landscape I'd ever read about.

"Don't turn," he said, once more behind me.

With effort, I didn't, but I scooted to the edge of the stair and angled slightly to press my shoulder to the banister posts. It was a compromise; I didn't face him, but I also didn't keep him directly at my back.

"What does it say?"

There was definitely more growl in his voice. Perhaps it increased with volume, and if he shouted, it would only be a wordless, bestial roar.

"It says, 'My name is Beauty.'"

"I knew that already." I heard a whisper of parchment, like he'd turned it in his hands. Did he have hands?

The silence stretched, but I was too full of music not to chatter. I kept my eyes focused on the steps below me as I spoke. "My mother, Rose, was a vain woman who valued handsome appearance above all other virtues. My eldest sister is named Astra, after the goddess. Next is Callista, after the queen. Isabella was stillborn, and when my turn came, I suppose all Mother's subtlety had been spent. So Beauty it is."

Again, silence. The castle's favorite occupant.

Perhaps he had gone.

I went on anyway.

"My poor brother." I forced a light laugh. "He was almost Narcissus, but Father wanted to have a son named after him, so Rob was spared Mother's terrible naming conventions. Luckily there was only the one boy."

This time, it was not silence that answered me. It was the most incredible sound I'd yet heard in the castle, a kind of quiet, rasping rumble.

It might have been a laugh. It must have been a laugh.

My smile blossomed, and my tongue ran away with every word that came to mind. "Beauty is a ridiculous name, of course. Mother would have been better to name me after a color. No matter how much there may be to admire about me in my mirrors, no one can live up to the bluntness of *Beauty*. At every introduction, no matter to whom, all that will be seen are my uneven ears or the point of my nose. If my name were Orange instead, perhaps someone would notice my eyes. Though were my eyes orange, rather than my name, they would certainly be noticed regardless of all else. So the true tragedy must be in my disappointingly un-orange eyes."

"You suit your name, Beauty," he said, quiet again.

I shivered, and not just at the rumbling pitch. I felt Stephan at my back.

"I have no name for you," I said quickly.

Another of his long pauses, then: "Beast will do."

"Very well, then. We shall both carry absurd names. If you wished to make the game more interesting, we could trade. I could be Beast and you Beauty."

That whispery laugh returned, and I forgot myself enough to look over my shoulder.

He vanished at my attention. I caught only the briefest glimpse—a snatch of black and purple, a flash of white. He was tall.

And then he was gone.

Stephan was charming at first, wealthy and mannered and possessing a sharp wit to match my own. We exchanged conversation with such ferocity, Callista mistook my feelings for hate and attempted to comfort Astra with the information. But I did not hate Stephan; indeed, I searched for him at every event, looked forward to the gleam that would enter his eyes when he spotted me.

"Well, my Beauty"—that was always how he greeted me. From there, we would dance through whatever topics we pleased, realistic or philosophical.

The first time he took dinner with our family, Astra tried desperately to catch his attention, starting a conversation in any way she knew how. Stephan turned each topic on its head, inviting debate that only I could answer, and before I knew it, it was a game, like we were throwing a ball back and forth over Astra's head as she jumped uselessly to catch it.

Both my father and Rob gave me stern glares at different points during the evening, but they could do nothing to wilt me. Not in Stephan's presence. We were an unstoppable force, one that could talk even my father into a corner.

Father was a man of God, a firm believer in monotheism, but together, Stephan and I looped the vines of pagan evidence around his legs until he had no more steps to take and admitted defeat with a troubled frown and a "We will all know the truth after death."

Even that, Stephan countered: "If death turns out to be the end of all things, we'll know nothing after it."

I should have considered my father's feelings, but I was preoccupied with the rush of victory and the thrill that came from Stephan's eyes on mine as we shared it.

"A man must live today," Stephan said, raising a toast to me. "Every untamable moment."

Every untamable moment—that was my romance with him. A wild burn of reckless indulgences as we broke society's rules and laughed. As the future baron, no one dared reproach him, and with me on his arm, no one dared reproach me.

No one except my brother.

"I don't like him," Rob told me bluntly after his visit to the house. "And I don't like who you are with him."

My face flushed, and I felt the betrayal as a dagger to my heart.

"Who I am with him," I said, "is who I *am*. Do you have

any idea what they say about me, Rob? The ladies of town. They say I'm a disgrace—to society in general, but specifically to Mother."

"You're not a disgra—"

"Oh, but I am. I'm whimsical. These women have children to raise, and I raise topics of what exists inside the stars."

"It's different," Rob insisted.

"It isn't," I shot right back. "With Stephan, I am free to be myself. And I shall be myself as long as I please."

No one could dissuade me, not Astra, not Rob. I continued forward in a reckless charge, lance of self-righteousness held high, never imagining the day would come when I would be unseated, left to be dragged behind my horse into the wild unknown.

CHAPTER 4

The wardrobe was insistent. Each time I passed it, the doors burst open, parading gown after gown of glittering, richly embroidered fabric for my consideration. At my refusal, the doors would snap closed once more, and the entire structure would wilt, sagging against the wall like an insulted maiden. Had it a wrist or a forehead, it surely would have thrown the two together in despair.

Yet had I ever been tempted by the offerings, my experience with the bath was enough to convince me that an enchanted dress would vanish off my form at the worst moment, leaving me naked. So to each of the gowns, I offered a firm, "No." I remained in my linen shift and dress, the pigeon among the peacocks.

If my host minded my attire, he made the same comment on the matter as he made on any other: absolute desolate silence.

No matter how I searched, the beast's whereabouts remained unknown. Each day, the castle was spotless, erasing any evidence that might have betrayed it was lived in. Even my own room was pristine each time I entered it.

"I am hardly intimidating," I whispered, after another futile foray into the endless castle looking for a door marked "Beast." I closed my own marked door gently—only just remembering to bolt it—and sat in the fading afternoon sun warming my window seat.

I should have been grateful for the solitude. My trip to the castle had been in search of the most complete escape, and the reality was as near as anyone could hope for. I was not only uneaten but undisturbed, and at my fingertips was anything I could hope to want. I had only to think of it, and the castle would pop it into existence.

But my desires were not so simple as silk gowns and savory pies.

I sat at the desk and wrote, *Your name is Beast.*

Then I took my place on the staircase and waited. Perhaps he would be angry that I continued to send messages he couldn't read. Perhaps today was the day to be devoured.

"Is it my name?" he asked.

I jolted upright at his voice. My fingers tightened on the edge of the stair beneath me.

"Yes." I licked my lips. "Your name is Beast."

Silence. That slight crinkle of parchment. He must have studied my earlier message enough to recognize the "name is" and, from there, to draw the conclusion as to the message's entire meaning. My instructors would have called him diligent, the same praise I'd enjoyed, and that was something, wasn't it?

"I'm surprised." My voice burst out of me without permission, itching to chatter. "Such a castle has a hundred expensive tapestries but not a single book. It isn't what I expected, especially knowing you can speak. Someone should have told you true wealth lies in learning."

He was silent.

And the itch returned.

"The benefit of wealth," I went on, "is that you can purchase learning, so in the end, I suppose true wealth is really wealth."

"I can't," he said softly, and his voice held that same tone he'd used at the gate. Broken. Cracked in a way that cracked my heart in return. It was worse than silence.

"Of course you can," I said brusquely. "The wealth in this castle could purchase anything in the world."

Even Father's fortune, laughable compared to a single rug in the beast's castle, had managed to purchase an education for all his children. Though far from grand, my education was extensive. Father ensured we were taught history, reading, and writing. Other instruction varied from child to child. For me, I had added music. And when it came to reading, I had far surpassed all my siblings; Astra and Rob had little taste for it, and Callista only enjoyed small doses of mythology or religious study.

"Are you angry to be here?" the beast asked.

"If a sow knew it was bound for slaughter, would it be angry?" I asked. "Who can say? If it volunteered for the act, we can only assume a resigned anger at worst."

The silence stretched so long, I was sure he'd left.

Then he said, "You're angry at something."

I stiffened, a fly pinned to the wall by its wings. And for the first time, I realized the fire inside was at least half ice, burning in a worse way until every part of me felt unnatural, inside and out.

"No harm will come to you here," the beast said. "The castle and grounds are yours."

No harm.

"I came for a punishment." My knuckles whitened. "I came to pay a debt."

"The loss of a daughter seems punishment enough. I am satisfied that you stay."

Father had been so certain. He'd told Rob: "He had fangs enough to tear a man's head off. I'm done for, son. I'm only grateful he granted me enough mercy to come home one last time."

"Don't return," Rob had begged.

But Father insisted he had no choice, that an enchantment would surely drag him back one way or another. He'd charged Rob with the care of the family, done everything short of lift the shovel for his own grave. Callista had wept nearly as hard as Astra. And I had . . .

"If you are satisfied so easily"—my voice held more snarl than his—"why demand punishment at all?"

The beast paused, then, "A prince must govern. Theft, however small, is theft."

I knew nothing of what he looked like, but he called himself a prince and spoke like a peasant.

"What are you prince of?"

Another of those absurd, stretching silences. He truly was a beast if it took such effort to gather his senses enough to hold simple conversation, especially when the response he finally settled on was a mere three words: "Only a castle."

This was not the bargain. This was not the fate.

But if I left now, Father would marry me off to Stephan, an attempt to ensure my safety that would instead ensure its removal forever. That beast had already been tested. At least the one standing at my back was still a mystery, even if I had rushed stupidly toward both.

"One stolen flower and you've sentenced yourself to my company for life." I draped my voice with amusement, better than any glittering gown. "It's a poor deal for you, I'm afraid."

"You do somewhat . . . confound me."

The honest admission startled me into a smile, then a laugh.

"You're not the first," I said quietly. Without thinking, I turned.

And he vanished.

Before the loss of his fortune, whatever I asked Father for, be it material or educational, he granted me. He was as indulgent with all his children as he could be, though he admitted that my requests were generally the most unexpected.

"Astra asks for things your mother cared for," he said. "Callista too, for the most part. But you have neither their interests nor mine. Philosophy, you said?"

"Like the great scholar, Archelaus." I snuggled into his lap.

"Wasn't he killed?"

"Stoned, yes. Because he taught that wealth disrupts the natural harmony of the world and should be forsaken. Rich people didn't like that."

"Can't imagine why," Father grunted. He wrapped his arms around me and sighed. "I don't care much for philosophy. There's no need for speculation that leads us away from God's commands."

"Oh, Papa, please!" I knew he couldn't resist when I called him Papa. "I can still pray even if I want to learn the limits of the universe, can't I?"

"So long as you remember that God has no limits."

"I remember, I remember."

He let me have my way, as he always did, and sometimes when my instructor came to the house, Father would sit by the door and listen. Never said a word, just listened.

"I'll admit," he told me, "I can't see the value in debating nothing, but it does my heart good to see you so diligent."

"It's not a debate of 'nothing,'" I said. "It's a debate of how nothing must come from nothing itself, and therefore—"

He kissed my forehead. "You're my daughter even if you confound me, Beauty. If it enlivens your mind, keep at it."

My instructor brought me stories and philosophies from the great cities. He had studied in schools with students of Archelaus and Cleo, and he taught me the importance of impartial, rational observation, of drawing my conclusions not only from my senses and experience but from the limitless space of objective possibility. I drank in every idea, read his writing and copied it in my own hand until every concept found a home in my mind and attitude.

Ironic, then, how Stephan slipped right in. I considered myself a master of rationality, but when it came to him, rationality played no part in my decisions.

Such as the evening Astra confronted us at the baron's harvest banquet.

Stephan and I had slipped away from the main event, and Astra followed us to a secluded balcony, her cheeks flaring as red as the sunset, though she usually tried so hard to maintain composure in Stephan's company.

"It's indecent!" she hissed at me, grabbing for my hand to pull me away.

But Stephan had my other hand, and of the two, there was no contest.

"Jealous, Astra?" he asked.

She released me like dropping a coal from the fire.

"I'm the eldest daughter, my lord," she said at last, the meaning clear. There should be no cause for jealousy. I could make no claim to a man until she and Callista had made theirs. Anything I experienced was stolen, rightfully hers.

I believe she half-expected him to realize the fault of his actions right there, to drop my hand as she had and take hers instead, apologizing all the while for every misunderstanding thus far.

But his answer was quite the opposite.

He drew me to him, our heat colliding in fire across my lips.

A rational mind would have remembered Cleo's theory of

harmful pleasures. A rational mind would have remembered that one swallow does not make a summer.

But the fire on my tongue burned out the rationality, immolated every word of wisdom in a heat that consumed me to my core.

CHAPTER 5

It was always cold in the castle. It had been summer at the cottage, heavy and warm, but the castle had the bite of spring in the air, increased with the onset of night. And with all that empty air inside the walls, any warmth that may have existed floated up to the vaulted ceilings and cradled painted cherubim, leaving me in the chill.

I sought sunlight where I could and fireplaces where I could not. My wardrobe offered me furs so bulky only a horse could be expected to carry them. I declined. It drooped.

"Maybe a shawl," I finally said, the admission a bit like pulling a tooth.

It presented me one of purple velvet.

"Maybe a real shawl," I amended.

Over the next several minutes, we haggled in a way that would have put even my father and his merchant colleagues to shame until the wardrobe at last spit out an unadorned woolen shawl. I thanked it so woodenly, we may both have been made of the same birch.

Nevertheless, the shawl was a big improvement. I wore

it everywhere, and despite my fearful expectations, it did not disappear. But the castle reassured me it was still enchanted through a much more grandiose gesture.

It produced a library.

I had wandered all the ballrooms, kitchens, studies, sunrooms, bedrooms, and even the dungeon. It was impossible I would have missed a library. Yet it sprang up on the same floor as my bedroom as if it had always been there, and I could not remember what it had replaced. Whatever it was, it was no loss to see it go.

The library was a warm room, full of the softest rugs and tallest windows, with bookshelves stretching high enough it required a ladder to reach their loftiest shelves, and when I first saw it, I sank to the floor and tried to pretend my eyes weren't burning with tears. Astra surely would have laughed in scorn to see me so moved by a collection of "overpriced firewood."

At the height of Father's fortune, we'd owned four books—three of them indulgences he'd purchased for me against better judgment when each one could have filled a wardrobe or started a dowry. Most of my reading had been done on borrowed materials or directly from the hand of my tutors, and I had been fortunate to receive such instruction.

All the tapestries, all the gold statues, every sign of wealth in the castle, this single room outshone them all. I'd never imagined so many books existed in the world.

I pulled them reverently from the shelves, pressed my fingertips to the ridges of the leather covers, stroked the spines. If I set one down, it floated back to its place and settled firmly on the shelf, as if the castle believed they were as decorative as the gilded portraits.

As if I would stand for that.

I clutched a volume of poetry to my chest, hunching to protect it from enchantments the same way I would protect it from rain. Then I sat in a red-cushioned armchair and sank myself into the words. At first, I read to myself, but some of the poems I murmured quietly aloud, enjoying the tinkling rhythm and rhyme.

It was then I felt the presence of another person in the room.

"Beast?" I swallowed, clutching the book to my chest.

The silence was not a guarantee he wasn't there. He might be measuring his thoughts, finding the words.

Sure enough, the rumbling voice came from behind me, so close I felt a tremor in the leather cushion against my spine.

"You may read aloud . . ." He hesitated, not content to reserve pauses only for between sentences. "If you'd like."

Listening was fine to gather information, but it would not help him learn to read the words himself. For that, he would need to see the words, to follow their shapes as I taught their sounds. Such a thing was impossible if he refused to let me see him. The only other way would be for me to copy a poem by hand, then have him read my copy on parchment as I read the original from—

Another leather-bound volume appeared in my lap, identical in size and coloring to the one in my hands. I thumbed its pages to be sure, but it was the same poetry from the same unknown author.

My knuckles whitened to see the book appear so casually, as if the original could be easily imitated, as if its value was a farce. I almost wished it gone.

"Beauty?"

He spoke my name softly, more rumble than letters.

"I need another book," I said. "I won't turn."

I set both volumes of poetry on the table beside my chair. One vanished while the other floated back to its place. I stood, careful to face forward and walk rigidly without turning.

On the second shelf from the door, I found a thin volume of folklore. The poetry had been dense and lofty, weaving music of the veiled sun who tried each day to descend to Earth only to be stopped by a lunar gatekeeper. I could have read it all afternoon, but it would not do for teaching.

Returning to the chair was no easy feat, but I felt my way carefully, head turned to the bookshelves, hand outstretched until I touched the leather of the high-backed chair. I eased myself into it and curled tightly, letting the softness envelop me like my father's arms had when I was younger.

At a thought, the book of folklore mirrored itself, and I stretched the second copy over the back of the chair without looking.

"Here." I willed my hand to stop shaking. "Read along."

My arm began to ache. The muscles pulled along my side, and just as I was about to drop the book in his stupid lap and relax my shoulder from its twisted, strained position—

His hand touched mine. The light brush startled me, and I did drop the book, but it was already in his hand. He had fingers, that was certain, though they were soft in the way of fur rather than skin. And something cold. A claw, or a claw-like nail.

I curled my arm into my sanctum once more. I could not run my finger across the page to show him the order; he would have to manage on his own.

"Left to right," I said.

And then I opened to the first story and read aloud to him of the man who mistreated his mule. The man would beat the poor animal whenever it reared its head against his command.

"I am master here," he reminded it with each strike.

While in the field one day, a bird dropped a golden seed on the man's hat. He planted it with his wheat, and come harvest, the wheat in that row all produced grains of purest gold.

"I am rich!" the man cried, sprinting to town to shout his news. In his absence, his poor abused mule trampled the entire row, and as each grain pinched between hoof and soil, it turned ordinary and useless, good neither as gold nor wheat.

"I am master here," the mule said.

When the man returned with a crowd of townsfolk eager to see his new fortune, they found only a trampled harvest and the mule missing. The mule found a new home with a family that never mistreated it, and the man wasted his life in drinking until he died, desolate.

"Not a happy story," the beast commented at the end, apparently too disgruntled to offer his usual pause.

If I tilted around the edge of the chair, would I see him sitting behind me, back pressed straight in a chair of his own? I resisted the urge.

"Happy for the mule," I said. "Folktales are almost always cautionary. Should I read something else?"

"No," he said, also immediate.

I smiled, and I turned to the next story, this one of the woodcutter who met a fairy. The fairy promised him three wishes, and with the first, he wished for great wealth. A storm of gold coins rained against his house, collapsing a corner of the roof and leaving him swimming in riches.

"I will buy a new house!" he cried.

For his second wish, he asked the fairy to make his wife the most beautiful woman in the world. Her thin, coarse hair turned luscious. Her skin gleamed more than porcelain. But his wife did not praise him for the change. She scolded him for using two wishes so thoughtlessly and for changing her appearance.

"She is an ungrateful crone," the man said, "and I wish her away."

It was his third wish. His wife vanished from existence, and the man hit his knees in regret. He begged the fairy for another chance, but she would not grant a fourth wish. He hounded her day and night, followed her through the woods in unbearable snows, and at last, in response to his wearying tears, the fairy offered a deal—to rescind all three wishes and for him to never again benefit from magic.

The woodcutter took the fairy's deal, and together, he and his wife shored up the broken roof of their tottering shack, living happily thereafter even if they were impoverished and ugly.

Or so the story insisted.

I gave a quiet, dry laugh after I finished.

"You dislike that one." There was a question in the beast's observation.

"They couldn't possibly live happily after that," I said. "And I doubt they lived happily before."

After a pause, he said, "It would be hard to forgive."

Impossible. By wishing his wife beautiful, the man had admitted he thought her ugly. Intolerable too, so much so that he wished her out of existence. Such a thing was impossible to forgive and certainly impossible to live with.

I felt Stephan looming at my shoulder, so I pressed back into the chair with all my strength, trying to press out the memory like oil from an olive.

"Do you think the woodcutter's regret was false?" Beast asked.

I'd been about to turn the page, to put physical distance between myself and the avaricious woodcutter, but the beast's question made me pause. I traced the words again in my mind, followed the woodcutter through the snowdrifts as tall as a man, watched the tears freeze to his cheeks.

In my experience, men didn't regret their greed, only the failure of it to procure what they desired.

But if the regret wasn't genuine, it was wildly foolish to sacrifice great wealth and magic only to share a run-down cabin with a plain woman the woodcutter despised.

"I don't know," I said, turning the page with finality. The memory of my instructor's lessons reared, reminding me of truth beyond bias. I swallowed, and as the new page fell, my voice ground out from between my teeth. "If he was willing to surrender everything he'd gained, our reasonable conclusion must be that his regret was genuine."

I thought that would be the end of the conversation, but the beast pressed on, surprising me.

"Suppose he later regretted the surrender."

It might have been my instructor there with me, goading me to the next thought, the next exploration.

I smiled. "Excellent point, Beast. You never mentioned you were a student of philosophy."

Something big shifted against my chair, tipping it forward a single degree, then settling. He must be sitting directly behind me, our spines separated only by leather and wood. If I reached over the chairback once more, would my fingers touch fur?

I cleared my throat. "Then comes the next question: If the woodcutter later regretted the surrender, was his initial regret therefore false? Perhaps motivated by a societal expectation? Or was this new regret false—born of wistful, temporary imaginings? Or were both regrets false together?"

The fireplace crackled, the only sound in the library. I realized the shadows in the room were slanting under the direct rays of a lowering sun. We would soon lose the light.

"Next story," Beast said, almost a plea.

I laughed. "I didn't mean to put you to the wringer, only to explore the debate." But something warmed my chest.

Had I been at home, no one would have asked me to examine the woodcutter's regret, much less kept up with a pursuit of such examination. Astra would have called it pointless, an invented speculation about an invented person. Callista would have taken the story at its word and only been frustrated at a cross-examination. Rob would have told me to believe what I wanted, that it made no difference to him. Father may have let me talk, but he would have made no contribution to the discussion.

"Thank you," I said, "for indulging me."

I felt Beast's weight press against the chairback, the gathering, and then the burst of speech, breathless yet forceful enough it shook the chair.

But it was not the force which scared me.

"Will you marry me, Beauty?"

My eyes widened. The book dropped from my slack fingers, but everything else in me tightened. I could feel Stephan looming above me, leaning to grip the chair arms, trapping me in his embrace, tying me up in his walnut curls. *Marry me, my Beauty.* No matter how I pulled at his arms, I couldn't move, couldn't breathe.

I screamed.

"Marry me, my Beauty."

It was his first proposal, and it pressed into my heart with all the weight of his fingers around mine.

"I'll be the baron; you'll be my baroness." His eyes gleamed. "Imagine it—every untamable moment."

I could imagine it, a lifetime of vivid colors and reckless charges with no one to hold us back. No one would dare call a baroness whimsical. I would have my heart's desire in books, in education, in sharp conversation with Stephan's insatiable mind. I opened my mouth to say yes.

And I thought of Rob. *I don't like who you are.*

Astra had not spoken to me since she'd witnessed our kiss. Perhaps she would never speak to me again.

I didn't care. Should Astra's bitterness keep me from happiness?

I don't like who you are.

It wasn't Astra's silence that bothered me. It was my reflection in a mirror. Even if Astra were the queen of perdition herself, I was no better to thrive in my spite.

"Stephan." I gripped his hands, willed myself to say yes. But instead I said, "If I were to marry before my sisters did, society would ridicule them. It would damage their future prospects. They would never forgive me."

"To hell with them and society both," he said.

It was certainly tempting. But I'd indulged in harmful pleasures long enough.

"Regardless, I have no desire to marry so young." A few more years at home, while I still fit on Papa's lap. "There is plenty of life ahead for us both, and untamable moments to spare. And you have your training to complete." He was under constant tutelage from the baron, preparing for all the duties that accompanied his inheritance. No one would recommend taking a wife in the middle of it.

There were times for recklessness. This was not one. I felt it with certainty, and I smiled under the calm rightness of the words on my tongue. Father would have been pleased with my decision and reasoning.

I didn't expect Stephan to be pleased, but he knew me so well, I knew he would understand.

He did not. And the cold that set in when he dropped my hands chilled to my very bones.

The beast heard my answer because my scream was not a wordless one, and I knew he vanished on the spot. I struggled to untangle myself from ghosts, managing at last to flee to my room. I should have run from the castle.

But where would a homeless girl go?

A dozen bolts appeared on my door, and though I slid each one into place, I felt no safer. Stephan had chased me to the cottage in the shadow of a forest and then to a castle isolated from the world.

No matter where I went, he would always be at my shoulder.

CHAPTER 6

I stayed in my room all the next day. When I played my violin, my fingers trembled. In the end, I curled around the instrument and let the sun wear out the day.

The next morning, my feet led me to the castle gardens. It was a dare, the same kind that had carried me to the heart of a dark forest in search of a bear. But that day, there had been no bear, and this day, there was no beast. For all the supposed harmony in nature, it would not balance out my unspoken desires.

The path led me to the golden gate, twisted in roses and thorns. Beyond it, the forest.

I turned away.

The gardens nearly encircled the castle, but there were other expected buildings—an armory, a livery stable. I entered the second, and a gentle chorus of whinnies greeted me. The stalls stretched as far as the dungeon cells had, an unimaginable cavalry for an empty castle. I stroked the nose of a chestnut mare. She nickered happily.

The horses were surely magic, and if I rode one, it would

disappear mid-gallop, sending me flying through the open air. Who knew where I would land?

I brushed and saddled the chestnut mare, and when I led her from the stable, a field had appeared between the gardens and the gate. Let there be an ocean of distance. I pulled myself into the saddle, settling the way Rob had taught me, and together we galloped. The mare never disappeared. Instead, she brought me right to that towering gate and its gold fence, stretching to the curve in the horizon. The longer I stayed in the castle, the larger it seemed to grow. Perhaps one day it would swallow the world. But somehow I knew the gate would always remain.

When I turned the mare's nose at the fence, she was heaving in breaths, so with a guilty heart, I dismounted and led her slowly until she'd recovered.

"Sorry, girl," I said quietly, stroking her neck. I moved to remount but halted.

The dark trees loomed like giants, reaching crooked branch fingers toward the tips of the golden fence posts. Somewhere in that forest was a fairy with eyes of larkspur blue. Had she given the beast his castle? Had she been the one to enchant him to speak?

I reached out like the branches, and as my fingertips touched the fence—

—she appeared.

She was small, no taller than the length of my forearm, and as she walked in the air, she left a glittering blue trail of footprints that lasted for a heartbeat before fading.

"Do you have a wish?" she asked.

Perhaps it was the suddenness of her appearance, or perhaps it was the foolishness of the question, but something about it struck me, and I laughed. Though my eyebrows lifted, the corners of my mouth did not because there was no real amusement in my strange laugh.

"A wish?" I echoed.

She smiled. "To every wish is given magic."

I thought of the broken teacup knit unnaturally back together. Stepping closer to the fence, I curled my hand around one of its gleaming posts.

"I didn't wish for the land to be cleared at the cottage," I said.

"My magic fulfills my own wishes as easily as it does for others."

"Why did you want to help me?"

To that, she gave no answer.

My throat seized. I pulled myself even closer. I could have slipped through the bars, but I only gripped them.

"Can you . . ." My voice broke. "Can you change the past?"

She tilted her head. "Do you wish to know?"

Everything appeared so easily in the castle. Barely a thought had caused a priceless library of books to take shape, and there seemed to be no cost, unless I had already unwittingly signed my soul away.

But a spoken wish to a fairy was different.

I thought of the woodcutter and his wife.

"No." I swallowed. "I make no wishes."

"Then you," she said, "are more stubborn than Wolf."

She disappeared as quickly as the beast did, though she left a set of shimmering footprints that followed her into nothing.

Slowly, I walked the mare back to the stables. *More stubborn than Wolf,* she'd said. The lack of an article pointed to a name, but I knew no one surnamed Wolf. In the end, it didn't matter if I was more stubborn than stone; I was still lost.

Was I wrong? I wondered, but there was no one to tell me. I thought of afternoons in my home, copying the writings of Archelaus as he taught balance in the world and "To everything, a cost." Some people believed he'd made a fairy wish to gain his wisdom. If so, his death may not have been the cost, but it was nevertheless the outcome.

Magic was an unruly thing. It could remake shattered porcelain without a scratch. It bent truth and reality to whatever obscene angles suited it. What if I wished to undo Stephan's attack on me only to find myself in a new future where events had veered in such a way that he'd convinced me to marry him after all and I was now his wife, chained to him body and soul, living out a nightmare for the rest of my days? I had to hold what meager ground I possessed, even if that ground was smoldering beneath my feet.

But just as I couldn't go back, neither could I go forward. At home, a reckoning was inevitable—whether brought by Stephan's reappearance or the observation of my family or the breaking of my own will, there would come a confrontation. And I couldn't face it.

What roared inside me could roar here with no one to mark it, and I had the space to ignore it. And maybe the same magic that held the castle flowers in eternal spring could hold me in place too, suspended between past and future, allowing me to curl in an unmoving corner and never be forced to walk the path forward again.

I looked up at the white towers piercing the sky, and the castle seemed more welcoming than ever.

It was another day before I encountered the beast again. I'd returned to the stables, and upon finding the same chestnut mare waiting for me, I'd named her Honey and claimed her as I'd claimed the violin.

Just as I reentered the castle after my ride and took the first stair toward my room, his voice came from around the corner.

"You don't have to stay."

Had I retreated a few steps, I could have perhaps seen him, pressed into the shadows against the wall. But I let the shadows be.

For a moment, I considered returning to the cottage, riding out of the trees on Honey. I saw Rob's shock, Astra's scowl. What would I say? In their eyes, I would be rising from a grave, and even the thought of telling them I was playing violin, eating fine food, and wasting my days in comfort while they worked their hands to the bone made me unable to lift my eyes.

And that wasn't even the worst part.

"Who would teach you to read?" I whispered. I cleared my throat, trying for an amused smile that simply wouldn't come. "I couldn't possibly leave a prince in such dire, uneducated straits."

"I don't understand," he said.

He didn't need to.

I climbed the next step, but his voice stopped me again. "I promised no harm to you. Do you trust that?"

This time I managed the wry, airy smile. "I trust no man's word. But a beast's may have a chance."

Then I took the staircase to my room and played my violin until I was certain the grooves in my fingertips would never fill again.

A throne room. That was what I realized was missing. All the kitchens, ballrooms, and even a library, but a palace without a throne room was no palace at all, and though I searched every room in the massive structure and walked staircases until my calves ached, I found no throne.

I did find a set of ornate double doors, arched to the ceiling and carved with the finest scrollwork. Beast's name was not engraved on either door, but it may as well have been.

They were the only doors in the castle that would not open for me.

Was he not permitted in my room even if he tried?

Or was I the only one locked from private quarters?

I thought about knocking. Instead, I took myself to the library and read aloud until I felt certain I wasn't alone.

"Do you live in the throne room?" I asked.

He made me wait for my answer as he always did. As if it were a hard question. But it must have been, because apparently, I'd confused him somewhere along the way.

"I live in the castle. But I have duties in the throne room."

Was it meant to be a jest?

"Duties?" I didn't mean to laugh. "Such as . . . what?"

"The duties of a prince."

He'd told me I confounded him. It couldn't be anything compared to how I felt concerning him. But the thought of prodding further felt like walking forward, and I'd determined to be content in my corner.

So I settled deeper into my chair and said, as if it were no matter of consequence, "I think I'll take my afternoons here. Reading. You're welcome to join, but don't let me keep you from your duties."

He said nothing, which was as good as agreement, I suppose.

After that, a pattern began to emerge. I used mornings as I pleased, sometimes taking my violin to the ballroom and sometimes playing to the birds outside my bedroom window. Here and there, I took Honey for a ride. Rarest of all was my practice in needlepoint. My creations were shaky and impatient at best, nothing like Callista's careful instruction and even less like Astra's pristine stitches and delicate knots.

Afternoons I reserved for the library. I always read aloud, and sometimes, a rumbling voice added keen observations during my pauses. And they were always keen; uneducated or not, the beast was not unintelligent.

"Can't I see you?" I asked once.

"No," he answered. He did not elaborate if the reason was magic or choice.

He never interrupted my reading, never stopped me to

ask the meaning of a word or passage, even after I encouraged it as my instructors had done with me. If he did not understand something, he kept it to himself, speaking only if he had a thought or wanted one from me. I found myself growing ever-maddeningly more curious about not only his appearance but also his mind—the questions and ideas he kept to himself. I had never wondered at anyone's mind before. Either they shared their thoughts as readily as I did, or I did not care to wonder.

In particular, I itched to know his thoughts on the swan who wished to be human.

It was the final story in the book of folklore, one I had heard before and always enjoyed. It was lyrical in its telling, more poetry than folktale, and I read with concentration, trying to give my audience an unbroken world of silent, longing song, without my tripping tongue to interrupt the picture of it.

The swan traveled far and wide in search of a fairy who would turn her human. Though no fairy revealed itself, she found in a broken temple the pendant of prayer, which granted the appeal of her heart. Her wings she traded for delicate fingers, her feathers for feather-soft skin.

She walked the harsh streets, her bare feet bleeding on the stone, and she saw cruelty she had never before witnessed, the betrayals and the beatings. The walking world was not as rosy as her yearning had made it out to be.

She looked back on her peaceful pond and saw with new eyes how it sparkled in the sun, how the frogs and reeds sang to the evenings, how there was as much good in her own world as was outside it. She dove deep into her pond's pristine waters and shook the pendant from her neck, leaving it to be buried in the sand. As she surfaced, she saw in her renewed reflection everything she could hope to be.

At the end of the story, I waited for the beast's observation, but none came.

"Beast?" I prodded. "What did you think of that one?"

But he only thanked me for reading, then disappeared for the afternoon. He never stayed long, but it still felt more abrupt than usual. Just to be sure, I peeked around the edge of my chair and found a cushioned stool, empty of its occupant, with only a creased indentation in the leather to show there had been a seat there at all. I smuggled the folklore book to my room with my violin.

After exhausting folklore, I introduced him to philosophers, reading passages on the ideas of origin and death, of the meaning of life and the lack of meaning in it. Scholarly writings seemed to be his least favorite, as he shared the fewest comments about them, although during one pause, he did say, "Now I know why you talk the way you do, with all the air."

My cheeks flushed. *All the air.*

"Whimsy," I said. "That's society's word for it. I am whimsical. Nonsensical. Impractical."

"I never said it was nonsensical." He always corrected me if I misinterpreted his meaning. "And if it is whimsical," he added, "then whimsy is welcome here."

At that, my cheeks flushed even more. I cleared my throat. The sunlight had taken on its usual farewell slant, and he would soon disappear, leaving me to return to my room for dinner alone.

"I'll take my meal here," I said abruptly. "Whether you stay or not."

It came out more obstinate than I'd intended, but I still felt the pressure against the spine of my chair. He didn't leave.

Without a word from me, a dinner cart zipped into the room, as easily as it always came to my sunny bedroom. There was a plate for me and a glass of fragrant wine, but nothing for him. My ears burned.

"Do you have your own cart?" How silly it felt to ask about dinner customs when they should have been obvious.

"No," he said, once more not elaborating if it was by magic or choice.

I'd once assumed he would eat me. The thought seemed ridiculous now. I could not imagine the keen beast who enjoyed folktales digging claws into wild game like a common wolf. But neither could I imagine him holding a fork if he could not hold a quill.

"You do *eat* . . . don't you?" My ears burned with double force. If only this had been a hypothetical discussion about a hypothetical talking beast, held in the safety of a schoolroom with my instructor.

"Don't let me keep you from your meal," he said, and I could swear the growl in his voice turned lazy at the edges, as if it had curved up in a smile.

I took it as a challenge, and as I dug into the food, I commented on every item I ate.

"These sweet potatoes are divine. Royal, I should say."

"I have never had a roast so juicy. It must be the favorite of a prince."

"Grapes from a king's vineyard, surely. Ah, I forgot where I was."

Each time I made one of my barbs, he had a ready answer for me, and with each one, I struggled to keep my face impassive. Sensitive to sweet potatoes, indeed, and no stomach for roast unless it was bone-dry.

"Beast," I said at last, "you are teasing me."

"Beauty," he said, "you teased me first."

And for a girl who didn't believe in miracles, such a thing came suspiciously close to being one. At first, I'd looked to him for escape, then to avoid the silence. Now I had to admit his company was enjoyable in its own right. Though he might have been a voice on the breeze or an invention of my own mind for all the evidence I had of him, I still looked forward to afternoons in the library.

As if to spoil that very thought, he said, "Beauty, will you marry me?"

I didn't drop my fork as I'd dropped the book. Instead, I clutched it all the tighter.

"Why?" I choked out, unsure what the question even meant.

I wasn't asking why he would want to marry me—he couldn't possibly want to.

I wasn't even asking why he was asking—first or second time—I only wished he would stop.

Perhaps I was asking the universe at large why the question existed, and why I could not escape it no matter how far I ran, not even to an enchanted castle buried in the middle of an impenetrable forest, a castle I couldn't leave for fear of the outside world.

If I began to fear the inside world as well, I would have nowhere left to go.

In the silence, my chest ached, and in my hand, the fork turned its tines toward me, everything pointed, everything exposed. If I said no, would he keep asking forever? Stephan hadn't. He'd asked three times, and then—

And then—

"I'll go," Beast said. "I'm sorry."

I thought of the woodcutter and his false regret. If the beast was sorry for asking, he wouldn't ask, certainly not twice.

I turned, ensuring the room was empty. Then in the fading light, I tucked myself deeper into the red armchair, pressing into its cushions, trying to dig myself a grave but finding no shovel to aid me.

Stephan's second proposal had come a fortnight after the first. He'd summoned me to the baron's estate alone, my cheeks turning pink as the servants gossiped about the cause. Nevertheless, I went, because it was Stephan, and if he called for me, it must be important. I thought perhaps his uncle had taken ill. Perhaps Stephan himself was ill. My stomach churned to think it.

But it was nothing of the sort. His second proposal was made before an audience of his two manservants, and though I tried to tell myself it was an oversight and not an attempt to add pressure, I could only think of the way he'd kissed me in front of Astra.

This proposal was more abrupt, more forceful, and when I turned him down, his anger increased as well. He demanded my reasons but was satisfied with none of them.

"I want to marry you," he insisted. "I love you. I thought you loved me."

"I do," I assured him, even as whatever feelings I did have wavered.

He fired accusations and arguments at me so quickly, I could not find my feet, until I grew confused of what I felt and wanted. He might have bullied me into accepting had he not been suddenly called away by the baron.

I slipped out of the estate without a word, even though he'd told me to wait for him.

After that, I began to avoid him.

After that, I began to fear.

CHAPTER

The next morning, I took Honey for a ride, and I led her right up to the fence again, staring through the bars to the forest beyond. The trouble with hiding in a prison was that it had holes. It was too easy for the outside air to come in; the cell was full of the stink of it. And it didn't provide any safety, only the feeling of being trapped.

I couldn't return to the cottage, but perhaps I could go farther. Perhaps I could climb aboard a ship and sail to the farthest corner of the world, where there was only undiscovered wilderness, where I could breathe deep the wet wilds and be so lost in fresh green there was no thought of old red.

But if I could get there, something could follow. I thought of my father's ships, lost in storms and taken by pirates. I thought of men much stronger than I, who had gone with solid hearts to salty graves, and I knew that, no matter where I tried to go, there would never be an escape to satisfy me. The escape I wanted was safety, a corner somewhere to tuck myself away in warmth and peace.

But there was no safety anywhere in the world.

I turned Honey's head from the gate, and we galloped through the field until the wind stung my eyes and left tracks of tears down my neck.

After lunch, my legs carried me to the library out of habit, but I paused at the threshold.

I looked at my armchair, at the muted rug and the fire already happily crackling. One hesitant step forward, but the heat from the fire was in the air, and it was heavy enough to choke. I pulled in on myself, hand to my stomach as I tried to breathe, but all I could feel was the heat.

I retreated to my room and curled on the window seat. The tray that brought me afternoon tea also brought a bowl of chilled water and a white cloth draped on the side. Thoughtful.

If an enchanted object is thoughtful, my instructor would have said, *is it the object itself possessing thought, or is it the compassion of he who owns the enchantment?*

"Quiet," I mumbled, pressing the soaked cloth to my neck and closing my eyes. Icy droplets chased each other down my collar, raised goosebumps across my skin. It calmed the roar, but my mind would never fully be silent, no matter how I begged it.

Instead, it wondered why I had been so unfortunate as to be born the youngest. Astra was seven years my senior, Callista five. Had I been in either of their places, perhaps I might have met someone before Stephan. Perhaps I might have walked a different path.

Yet my mind would not even allow me to content myself in daydreams, reminding me neither Astra nor Callista had found such fortune, and suppose I had married a man, but one who multiplied Stephan's brutality. Were such a thing possible, I surely would have walked into it with naïve eagerness. The path I'd taken to arrive here only confirmed that.

I wasted the day in paralyzing hypotheticals until, in the evening, a sheet of parchment slid beneath my door, floating across the carpet like a boat on waves until the tide brought it to rest beneath my bench.

My cloth had lost its chill, and my left leg had gone numb beneath me. It needled painfully as I uncurled. I lifted the parchment into my lap and saw the same thick, shaky lines that had first directed me to my room, only now they weren't employed in art. They were employed in letter writing.

MY NAME IS BEAST

His letters were hopelessly crooked, collapsing in on one another like new fawns all struggling to walk. Still, he'd taken my first message and my second and structured a new sentence all his own. He understood the heart of it.

For all Stephan's intelligence, he'd detested writing.

"I'll hire a scribe," he said, "or I'll speak in person. My time is too valuable to be wasted on parchment."

It was the patience required that he detested. Stephan was a man of quick mind, quick tongue, quick results.

Beast was not. He was not even the type to rush the gathering of two words.

I sat at my polished writing desk, and directly under his sentence, I rewrote the same letters as neatly and unembellished as I could, emphasizing the straight backs and smooth curves. Then I let it float back to him.

He took the hint and returned a second attempt. There was not much improvement, but I could see the effort. For the rest of the evening, we traded that sentence, passing the ball back and forth with gentle correction and patient obedience. He never rushed a reply, and his calm meticulousness calmed me in turn until the storm inside me gave way to the quiet rhythm of my heart and the echo of that repeated message: *My name is Beast.*

During one of our afternoons in the library, he'd asked the nature of my family.

"Where to begin," I'd said, smiling ruefully. "With the eldest, I suppose, and in order. Rob is clumsy and in love. Astra is selfish but talented. Callista is mischievous, and her interests change with the wind. Then there's the youngest of the family—she is whimsical and, overall, quite useless." He might have contradicted me had I given him a chance, which I did not. "The family has, of course, two parents, as families do. Father is thoughtful and hardworking. Mother succumbed to a fever several years ago."

At the description of my mother, he observed, "Hardly a trait."

"You're correct." I had to wrestle my memory, to wring from it things I'd set aside either by intention or accident. "Mother was vain, as I've said. Questionable judgment, particularly in naming her children. An upstanding woman of society." I remembered her in the sitting room, laughing with friends. I remembered the way Father's face always softened when he said her name: *Rose.*

"She pitied the ugly and the poor, but unlike her friends, she did not do so with inaction. Our kitchen frequently extended meals to servants and strangers alike, and although it was beneath her to be a seamstress for work, she employed the skill for charity."

My chest ached, and I finished quietly, "Astra fancies herself Mother's image in every way, but she has only the beauty and vanity without the generosity."

The beast gave his usual pause, as if revisiting each of my words before drawing his conclusions.

In the end, he surprised me by asking, "Do you take after your mother?"

"Not in any way. Did you not hear the generous description? Nor am I my thoughtful father's child except in blood. I am an ugly, degenerate apple, unbeholden to any tree."

"A beast," he said simply.

Unexpectedly apt. And in the following silence, I felt companionship, until my restless soul could bear the stillness no longer and I returned to reading.

Now, several evenings later, I felt that companionship all over again.

My name is Beast.

The next day, I returned to the library with determination. I curled up in my chair, and I started reading. As soon as I did, somehow, I knew he was there. I closed the book and waited, scratching my hand to keep my attention focused so I wouldn't fill the silence with mindless chatter.

"Why do you stay?" he finally asked.

"I thought about sailing," I said. "But I have no sea legs."

I tried to wait again, but my heart jittered with each moment, turning my breaths unsteady until finally I choked out, "Please don't ask me again. If I'll . . . The question you asked the other day."

"I'll try not to," he said quietly, which was a ridiculous response.

"I intend to die alone." I tried for amusement but gripped my book too tightly, creaking the leather. "I won't marry anyone. Ever. So there's no point in asking."

"Alright."

He sounded neither defeated nor rebellious, and my uncertainty only increased the rate of my anxious heart.

"If you have any ideas about—about forcing me—"

"Never!"

My chair scraped forward under the force of his protest. It was the first time he'd ever cut me off, the first time he'd spoken without seeming to need any thought. Intellectually, it was comforting. But in the empty room before me, I saw Stephan at every corner.

"Well, you are a beast," I said. "All men are. Reaching for roses that aren't theirs."

That was the reason I was here, the reason for all of it. Stolen roses.

After that, we didn't speak, and I read in haunted silence.

Father told us it was a storm unlike anything he'd ever seen. He was still pale, trembling so much he couldn't hold the cup Callista tried to press into his hands. In the early years of building his fortune, he'd been a seafarer, so he described it as a hurricane, but rather than the salt-sting of ocean water and the wild roll of waves beneath a ship, this was the roll of once-solid earth beneath his feet and the stinging lash of branches in the wind.

And then the castle.

"White as heaven itself," he choked out.

A refuge from the forest, with gates that swung open before he even thought to enter them. He called out for the owner, but there was no answer, not even from a servant. Only food laid at a table and bandages for his bleeding hands and face.

"You should have run!" Astra said.

He told her he would not have survived the storm, but she was unsatisfied with the feeble excuse.

When he did work up the courage—or the fear—to leave, he did not make it out.

Because the path to the gate wound through a rose garden.

"Stunning," he whispered, gazing right through his gathered children as if he could still see the rose bushes beyond. "Filled the air with every . . . every color imaginable."

Apparently the color he'd chosen to pluck was pure gold.

I turned the rose in my hands, every petal exquisitely formed and gleaming, the heft of it like a lead weight against my fingers. It was impossible to imagine it had come from a living bush, but no more impossible than a fairy in the woods.

Father hadn't returned from the forest with meat, but what he had returned with would buy food enough to last the winter and beyond. Surely there had never been a more successful hunt.

I smiled.

But the pit of my stomach burned.

And in my father's shadow, I saw Stephan's curls.

CHAPTER 8

This time, I didn't take Honey to the fence. I walked on my own, and I brought the book of folklore. I sat by the fence as I sat by the fire in the library, and I read aloud the story of the woodcutter.

When the fairy appeared, I saw the sprinkle of blue sparks out of the corner of my eye, but I kept reading without pause.

"You have to trap a fairy first," Callista had said as she was explaining to me every reason our land couldn't possibly have been cleared by a fairy. "Once captured, they have to grant a wish. That's the only way to get magic. Otherwise, all they'll do is talk about themselves."

The fairy had offered me a wish without capture, so there was no guarantee Callista's analysis was correct in any other aspect. Yet in my brief conversation with the fairy at the fence, the only straight answer I'd received had been about her own desires, so the hypothesis was worth a test.

And sure enough—

"Preposterous," she spat, stomping a blue foot as I read about the woodcutter's second wish. "If he wished for his wife to be the most beautiful woman, he would receive the most beautiful woman. Not a transformation of his current wife."

"Interesting." I directed my thoughts to the air, not letting my gaze confront her directly. "Both are valid interpretations."

Yet fairies were notorious for trickery.

She sparked like a tiny flash of lightning and stepped closer as if to confront me. "Acceptance is acceptance. A wish is a wish."

She said it as if it made perfect sense, but I imagined even my instructor would have had difficulty parsing her meaning.

"If he wished to have never met his wife"—I struggled to maintain a tone of intellectual curiosity—"would he return to an empty house or to one where his wife greeted him at the door and he had no memory of her?"

"Both are nonsense. There would be no house."

Her circling riddles were maddening. While the heated knife inside threatened to fillet my skin from bone, I forced a slow breath.

Even if I could draw a straight answer, a hurdle still remained.

To everything, a cost.

I flipped the page. "When the woodcutter wished for wealth, the rain of coins caved in his roof. That must have been the fairy's price for the wish."

She sighed with such force that she cast a waterfall of shimmering stardust to the ground. "The result of a poor delivery system and a thoughtless granter. Regret is the only price for wishing."

Regret.

I swallowed. "Should I read the end?"

"Do as you like." She kicked a bit of blue glitter into the air, turning her nose up. "It's a foolish story."

But she didn't disappear.

I returned to my oration, following the woodcutter through his third wish, his regret, and his diligent chase.

"A granter can only be found," the fairy grumbled, "if the granter allows the finding."

When the woodcutter had his wishes rescinded and I finished the tale, I waited for her to spark like lightning again. But she only said, "What silly ideas."

Which ideas seemed silly to me likely differed from the ones that stood out to her.

"I'm sure fairies don't rescind wishes," I said, pretending at certainty on the matter.

"We can't," she said. "Only completion can."

"Completion?"

She turned suddenly, squinting at me as if I'd just leapt from the bushes or revealed a true form.

"Have you a wish?" It sounded more like an accusation than an inquiry.

I'd been found out.

My ears burned. She'd said there was no price but regret.

Would I regret it?

I waited too long, and she vanished.

My feet dragged as I returned to the castle. The spring air felt wet and heavy in my lungs. I stopped in one of the gardens to sit on a stone bench in the shade of a blossoming tree, and I buried my head in my arms. For once, my racing mind was hushed, everything inside pressed quiet by the weight.

It hurts, Mama. It was what I'd told her at my first bleed.

It won't hurt forever, she'd said.

But wouldn't it?

Something chirped. I lifted my head and turned to see a fledgling bird in the grass. It fluttered wildly from side to side, mostly just scraping its face as it tried to move forward. Probably injured. It chirped again.

"Not me," I said. I was no caretaker; I had spite in my soul. Let its mother come.

Its mother.

I was surrounded by her—gold roses in the gate, red roses in every garden. Carved on my door, carved in my heart, the scent in every aching breath.

Will I regret it, Mama?

Regret was the fire in my stomach, melting my bones but without the courtesy to finish me off. Every day burned me down to embers, and there was relief when dark descended and my head hit the pillow. Except the embers didn't die in the night. Instead, the night dragged in fuel, and come morning, I was fresh and ready for burning all over again. Never consumed. Never an end.

He haunted my dreams worse than he haunted my days. Sometimes with a different face or in a room we'd never entered, but always with the same heat and the weight of his body on mine.

Never an end.

My eyes burned. Everything burned. A fire along every raw nerve, the heat of his touch was never extinguished, only sank deeper and deeper and deeper. My fingernails pierced my skin. My breaths hitched in my narrow throat.

I looked at the bird once more.

It fluttered and struggled alone.

And then my fingers fluttered as I reached out to lift it. It squawked and twisted, probably terrified to be held by a grip it couldn't escape. I nearly dropped it at the thought, but I held on, rotated it and saw that one leg was a stump. The castle grounds seemed to house no predators, so it must have been born at a disadvantage. Or perhaps there were predators I could not see. It would not be the first time.

I found its nest in the overhead tree branches, then returned it gently. But I knew it would fall again. Because what was lost would not regrow, and it would continue to struggle, so there was nothing to do but fall.

It hurts, Mama.

That afternoon, when I went to the library, my chair had been moved.

Rotated, more accurately. Turned to face the window. I couldn't see its occupant, but I saw a thin line of purple velvet at the arm. A pair of pointed black ears rose above the tall chairback, one of them flicking sideways at my entrance.

I stared in shock at the most evidence I'd ever had of the castle's only other occupant.

"What are you doing?" I finally asked, unable to help my nervousness at any change.

In answer, he started reading.

Beast's voice was halting, and he read slowly, stumbling over easy words. Some he skipped entirely or mispronounced in such a way I could only glean the meaning from spotty context. Nevertheless, I stood and listened, and my smile grew with every sentence. He was reading from the book of folklore, the story of the man and the mistreated mule.

It was a mere two pages; it must have felt like eternity to him. I was not so far removed from my initial lessons that I'd forgotten how daunting a full page seemed at first. But he persevered through the entire story, and somewhere along the way, I claimed the stool he usually sat on and placed it behind the chair so I could sit with my back against his as I imagined he did to me when I was the one reading.

I listened to his rough voice, to the catches and little snarls, and I wondered if it was only the result of reading around fangs or if what I heard was some hint at a rural dialect. Faint vibrations reached through the wooden chairback to me, and for some reason, there was comfort in feeling his voice against my shoulders.

When the story ended and he fell silent, it seemed too soon.

"Now I'm convinced we should switch our names," I said, smiling.

"You mock me."

"I don't." I didn't want him to think that. "I enjoyed listening. Truly."

I heard the gentle rustle of the book closing. Then he said, "I never knew it dried out your mouth."

"With practice, that eases. You'll find a rhythm."

"I imagine it will take years of practice." But he didn't say he wouldn't do it.

He'd shared something with me. Something vulnerable.

"Do you enjoy music, Beast?" I hoped he couldn't feel my pounding heart through the chair.

"I do."

"Wait here."

I hurried down the hallway to my room and gathered my violin and sheet music.

When I returned, my chair was empty and once again in its usual orientation, but I could still see the flicker of black ears behind it. I settled with straight posture and concentrated on my instrument, fiercely telling my roiling stomach to be calm as I tried *not* to imagine each book an enchanted audience member.

My largest performances had only ever been at dinner parties, and most of them held within the first few years of my learning, with sweet pats on the head from the little old ladies of society to encourage me. I played the violin for myself, not for any acclaim, so my family, my tutor, and the walls of my own home had been my only repeated audience.

In fact—

Stephan had never heard me play.

Realizing that brought an increase of air to my lungs, and it was enough to settle the violin against my shoulder and draw the first down-bow. The mournful opening echoed in the room, easing my tension. Soon enough, I'd forgotten I had an audience at all and played as I did in my bedroom, with no goal but to hear the music and feel it vibrate my heart.

After the last piercing note faded, I lowered my instrument to choose a different song and was startled to hear gentle thumps, which took me a moment to identify as quiet applause from fur-lined hands.

My face heated. I coughed.

"Will you play another?" he asked.

I wished I could tell from his voice if it was a personal request or just a societal expectation.

Either way, I lifted my bow for the next piece. And the next.

"It can't be exciting for you." I lowered the instrument to my lap between pieces to give my arms a needed rest for blood flow. "You listen to me talk, listen to me read, listen to me play. I feel selfish."

I was known for dominating the conversation at home, and I'd been called out at many social functions for an impatient, tapping toe when I was meant to be listening to imparted wisdom from others.

"Maybe you are selfish."

I winced at his unrelenting honesty, but I'd walked myself into it.

Then he added, "Maybe I am also selfish, since I ask you to speak, to read, and to play for my own enjoyment."

So it had been a request. I ducked my head, massaging the tired fingers of my left hand to distract from the tingling in my chest.

"I hope you won't be embarrassed." I wasn't sure what made me say it except that honesty deserved honesty. "If you don't want to be seen, it's your right, but I hope you won't be embarrassed. No matter how you look, you offer good and honest conversation, and that's more than most people do."

We were dangerously close to something I hadn't allowed myself to ponder, but despite my resistance, my instructor's voice prodded me: *Is it a beast who speaks like a human or a human who looks like a beast?*

"There is a fairy in your forest," I said, rushing into a new topic.

I felt his stiffness all the way through the chair.

"She offered me a wish."

"Don't take it!" he said, suddenly fierce.

"Did you?"

More stubborn than Wolf, she'd called me. I couldn't help thinking of his pointed, black ears.

The silence grew. Perhaps he couldn't tell me, couldn't speak of it. I was certain I could reason it out, and the prospect of such a puzzle should have thrilled me. It would have thrilled the old Beauty.

But this one was in hiding, and down the path ahead of me, I saw only exposing light. The beast had secrets, but so did I. Best to leave secrets in the dark.

"Beauty—" He stopped abruptly, with such effort my chair tipped a few degrees forward, jolting my heart.

I could guess what he'd been about to say.

When I'd told him not to propose again, he'd said he would *try* not to. My irritation had heard only Stephan in the answer, a man unwilling to surrender what he wanted. I hadn't heard enchantment.

Now I did.

I hugged my violin. I'd foolishly opened a door, and the wind had blown in grains of truth I couldn't sweep back out.

Don't ask, I ordered myself. I didn't want him to know what I'd put together if I was right—and I felt horribly sure that I was.

If he was under an enchantment that only a marriage agreement could break, he had the wrong girl in his castle. Astra could have married him; she would be happy to marry wealth regardless of feelings. But perhaps the castle would vanish with his enchantment. Perhaps every benefit would vanish, and his good temper too, and all that would be left would be the soulless chains of marriage to a true monster. Perhaps he was a wicked man who'd been transformed into a gentle beast. It would fit a fairy's sense of twisted humor and irony.

There were too many possibilities for me to guess at the truth, and I owed him nothing. I owed nothing to any man. I couldn't—

I realized there was something different in the silence.

"Beast?"

He was gone.

CHAPTER 9

In my room that evening, a sheet of parchment arrived. Beast had copied down the line about the woodcutter's regret, and I couldn't tell if he was answering my question about a fairy wish or simply apologizing for trying to propose again.

I tucked the parchment away in my desk, and I tried to tuck my inquisitive mind away just the same.

The next day, I halted on the threshold of the library and turned my steps to the gardens instead. I walked the fragrant paths, reaching out to brush my fingertips across velvety petals, and when I sat on a bench, I felt a familiar presence behind me.

"Why do you love roses so much?" I asked.

"I don't."

I stiffened. "My father's punishment was for taking a rose. The door to my room has roses carved beside my name."

"The castle draws people in," he said at last, and there was almost an apology in his tone. "It chose your room."

"But you were the one who threatened my father."

Silence. Then, in that same apologetic tone, "I was."

I was getting too close to the truth again, investigating without meaning to.

Grabbing at a different track of conversation, I said, "I was not surprised when he brought it home. The gold rose. Father is hardworking, but he revels in what his hard work brings him. He pretends he has recovered from losing his fortune, that he can be content with a country life, but the greed is still in his eyes, and even after all the hospitality of the castle, he could not resist the glint of it on his way out."

It was too much to ask a man to resist the beauty before him—Stephan would have said that. He would have said it was my father's right to take what he wanted by force. He would have said the rose had deliberately planted itself in my father's path to tempt him.

"Men fall for the sake of a rose," I said. "Perhaps that is why I prefer the company of a beast."

I took the path again in silence. I expected him to leave, but I continued to feel his presence at my back, and I heard the gentle disturbances of footfalls on the ground behind me and the brush of reaching plants against a moving form. So I walked without looking back.

I had finished a circuit of the buttercups and the lady's mantle before Beast spoke again.

"The rose was not gold when he took it. It looked . . . ordinary."

"Don't say that," I murmured, heart tightening.

If I could write off my father's act as greed, it was easy to stay in the castle, not missing him. If I could pretend Stephan's failings were shared by all, I could keep all at arm's length.

But if they insisted on being human, on being complicated, I would have to pick through the pieces carefully, see the intentional harm when I didn't understand it, try to find where the cracks had begun, wonder if I should have noticed them sooner. I would pick through the tray of glass fragments until every piece was slick with blood and I could no longer see the edges and I was no closer to understanding and all I felt was the pain.

I came to a stop on the path. "My mother." I clenched my jaw, drew in a breath. "He thinks of her whenever he sees them."

Papa was a literal man, not a cruel one, and his love for my mother was genuine. I had never expected that fact to make me shrivel inside, to make me feel bitterness rather than hope. But I had simmered long enough to go sour. The rot was so deep in my soul, I saw it everywhere. I saw greed and cruelty where it did not belong—in my father, in my brother.

In the beast.

Just then, he said my name, soft and barely audible.

I waited.

"You can turn," he whispered.

I would find more truth if I did, truth I couldn't sweep out.

Nevertheless.

I turned so slowly it felt unnatural, the deliberate creep used to avoid startling a frightened child. I kept my eyes on the path first, for both our sakes, so I saw first that he did not wear boots. They would not have fit his feet, bent as they were like an animal's, built for powerful leaps to take down large prey.

With that same slowness, I raised my eyes.

He must have worn his purple velvet suit as I wore my plain dress, with stubborn devotion, and that was enough to almost make me smile. It wasn't so bad—he wore a suit because his shape was mostly human, with the expected torso and limbs, even if they had unexpected claws and joints. Without boots, his pant legs hung loose below his knees. There was white lace trim on the hem and cuffs of his jacket.

In the direct sunlight, his fur was a rich hickory brown, not black, and it covered any skin that would have otherwise been visible—his feet and hands, his neck and chest where his suit hung open without an undershirt.

And his face.

He tensed as my eyes met his, drew back a full step.

For a moment, I thought he would bolt, so I whispered, "Don't go."

I remembered his voice saying the same to me when I'd first come to the castle.

I'd heard a legend of werewolves once. It was not a tradition in our country, but nevertheless, it was what came to mind. There was certainly wolf in his pointed ears and muzzle, in his large round eyes and black nose. His fangs were visible in the tiniest spot of white beneath his slightly parted, tensed lips. It must have been hard to read aloud, hard to speak. Yet he did it for me.

"Alright," I said. I didn't know what else to say.

Then he disappeared. One moment there, the next only empty path and flowers nodding gently in the afternoon breeze. I supposed he'd shouldered my gaze as long as he could bear.

And just as I'd expected—

It was impossible to go back.

Beast did not come to the library the next afternoon. I waited to hear his voice, pausing more and more often until I couldn't even finish a full paragraph before I was checking for his presence. I finally reached up, but all I felt was the smooth wood of the chairback. When I peeked, the space behind me was empty, not even his stool.

For a few moments, I just stared.

Then I set my book aside and climbed the stairs to those massive double doors that wouldn't open for me.

I knocked. Pitiful. Barely a sound against the wood, absorbed in the density of two massive doors that could have admitted giants, yet it left my knuckles red. I knocked harder.

"Beast," I called out. "Can I . . . come in?"

The sconces along the hallway trembled. I'd thought everything in the castle had finally adjusted to me, but this was only my second visit to this particular landing.

He'd told me he had the duties of a prince to attend to, and I'd brushed him off. My cheeks reddened now to think of it. How many times had I been brushed off the same way? Whimsical Beauty. Who was I to judge a strange prince?

Royal responsibilities in an empty castle seemed ridiculous, but so did a gold rose, so did a blue fairy.

With purpose, I cleared my throat and stepped back. Squaring my shoulders as evenly as I could, I curtsied to the guarding doors.

"I seek an audience with the prince," I declared.

Just like that, the doors split, impossibly silent despite their size, like everything in the castle. As they swung inward, the air snaked between them and caught my legs with reaching fingers, pulling me forward.

I stepped into an immense, cold room, lined on either side by white pillars and vaulted arches with braided stonework. The gray ceiling was higher than any other in the palace, chandeliers dangling above every second arch.

But the true light in the room came from the windows, and I gasped. Instead of the golden sunlight that usually spilled through the tall glass, it came in every color, as varied as the flowers in the gardens—diamonds of blue and green, squares of yellow and purple, angled petals of red, all jumbled together and stretched across the white floor like a tumbled basket of fruit.

I walked through the center of the room, extending my arms to see the color paint my skin. The windows themselves created pictures from the color, vibrant images of royalty and what must have been angels, all lining the path that pointed to a throne on a raised dais.

Straight-backed and unyielding, the seat was framed in gold. It was too tall for any person, yet taller still was the banner hung above it: a snarling black wolf's head on a purple background. Somehow, I doubted Beast had chosen the crest himself. He seemed more the type to prefer a swan.

Beast was not seated on the throne; he was not on the dais at all. He stood at a table below it, and he flinched when my eyes found his.

He didn't speak, so that duty fell to me. It was never such a struggle in the past.

"It's my crops," I said at last, the only words I could scrounge up.

"What?"

Though we were separated by only a table, both of our voices echoed in the expansive room.

"I sought an audience with royalty, didn't I? It's my crops, Your Highness. That's the problem."

At home, I would have expected an eye roll. Maybe a dismissive gesture or a resigned nod allowing me to do as I pleased. But Beast generally surprised me in his responses, and I was hoping he would surprise me once more.

He did not disappoint.

"Oh," he said evenly. His gaze darted in my direction as he added, "It must be serious."

"Terribly serious."

"What seems to be the problem?"

"They've run away."

He turned aside, hunching as if he could hide his tall frame behind the table, but I thought he might have been smiling.

"Serious indeed," he said.

One of his hands was curled over the edge of the table, and for a moment, I lost myself staring at the thick, black claws below the lace of his sleeve. Then I forced myself to look at his face, even if he wouldn't look at mine.

"I'm sure you know this is very rare for crops." I shook my head. "My neighbor's wheat never makes him chase it down, yet my potatoes have been unruly from the moment of planting. Shifty-eyed, every one of them."

Beast gave a quiet cough that must have been a laugh, and if he wouldn't turn, at least he hadn't disappeared.

"How can I help?" he asked.

A strange prince indeed.

"I thought you might order them back to my fields. Perhaps a royal decree that, in this kingdom, the desertion of potatoes from their rightful plantings will not be tolerated."

"Maybe I support freedom of potatoes in this kingdom."

Teasing again. I smiled. Without thinking, I stepped to the closest edge of the table, and when my gaze took in its surface, I raised an eyebrow.

"What's this?"

A long scroll had been pressed flat across the table's length, held down by small weights in each corner. I thought at first it might be a game because it was littered with chess pieces, until I realized each piece bore a pennant—some purple, some green—and the scroll itself was patterned with the curves of hills and the paths of rivers. The pieces moved by an invisible hand, grouping and separating.

Beast said, "Military strategy, I think."

"Military?" My eyes widened. "Is there a whole army stashed away in some corner of this castle?"

Would it be any more surprising than the rest of it?

I watched the pieces slide across the map. There was no sense to my eyes, and I wondered if the meaning was clear to him. But his yellow eyes watched the table without betraying any more of his thoughts than when I'd had only his voice in the air.

"Ah," I said at last, rapping my knuckles against the table's edge as if I'd hit a discovery. "So *this* is how one is meant to conduct an assault against unruly potatoes. Very helpful, Your Highness, thank you."

"Ah," he said in return. "So that's what it was."

I was no longer sure what characters we were playing.

"Come to the library tomorrow," I said, surprising myself. "I don't like reading to an empty room."

He held my gaze for the briefest moment.

And then he nodded.

CHAPTER 10

Stephan hunted me down to make his third proposal.

I had gone to town with Callista. She had begged Father for a new dress for the upcoming ball at the baron's estate, hoping she might catch the eye of some eligible young man, although where she was going to find one she hadn't already met, I did not know.

I dreaded the ball with each day that brought it closer, and while Callista was measured and fitted, I waited on the street, wondering if I should fake illness to avoid the event. No one would believe me if I simply said I did not wish to attend, not when I'd sought every opportunity for Stephan's company in the past.

As if summoned by my thoughts, he appeared on the street with me. The pounding of my heart at his company was not exhilaration. I tensed, expecting more anger and railings.

But he came to me instead with tears and apologies.

"I'm sorry," he said. "I don't know what I did to make you lose faith in me."

"I'm sorry," he said. "I don't know why you think I'd make such a terrible husband."

And with each word, the guilt gnawed in my stomach until I was apologizing along with him—*You aren't terrible, Stephan. I love you, Stephan.*

I thought we'd reached an amends, that everything before had been a misunderstanding, and this was the edge of a new page.

Until he said, "Beauty, I cannot live another minute without you as my wife. Please."

It *was* the edge of a new page.

But not the one I'd hoped for.

Instead, I felt the slicing realization that he was buying me with false contrition the way Callista was buying gowns with coins.

When he took my frozen silence as agreement to his proposal, the quick melting of his tears into satisfaction proved the insincerity.

"I won't marry you, Stephan," I said, so detached from my own voice that it no longer sounded like mine at all. "Not ever."

His satisfaction turned to anger. He called me vain. He called me selfish. Only a great fool would refuse such a husband. My father would be ashamed, he said. Robert Acton had grown a fortune from dirt only for his daughter to turn up her nose at every opportunity offered her. Without Stephan, I would wind up back in the dirt, and it would still be better than I deserved.

Father wouldn't be ashamed of me for refusing.

Would he?

When I tried to think of him, all I could think of was Astra. She would consider anyone a fool to refuse Stephan.

Long after Stephan's voice faded, a few of the barbs remained, tiny slivers festering in a once-confident mind.

Callista came bursting out of the seamstress's home, calling for me, and Stephan turned to greet her as cheerfully as if nothing had happened. She squinted at the two of us having a private moment, and I could see in her eyes assumptions that churned my stomach. After Stephan left—with a lingering look at me—she reminded me none-too-gently that Astra was still without a husband.

"You can't imagine how she feels, Beauty." Callista heaved a sigh. "To be twenty-four and unmarried."

And Astra could not imagine how I felt, to be seventeen and cornered by a man I'd thought loved me. Had I been twenty-four at his first proposal, I would have accepted it, and perhaps I never would have seen his anger until the contract had been signed.

"Basing marriage on age is foolish," I said. "If she cannot find a *good* man, then better to be forty and unmarried instead of twenty, married, and miserable."

Callista rolled her eyes and told me that, in a few years, I would understand.

"Or maybe you never will," she added wistfully. "Beauties always marry young."

She was a beauty. Astra was a beauty. Beauty had nothing to do with it, yet people always used it as a dart against me thanks to my terribly unsubtle name.

I was unlucky, and I'd caught the eye of a demon. But if I tried to tell Callista as much, she would roll her eyes and sigh. Whimsical Beauty, conjuring fanciful ideas. I was always the young, naïve one who would eventually learn the true way of the world.

So I told no one.

And I tried to manage Stephan on my own.

Although Beast let me see his face now, he kept his distance when we shared a room, and if there were shadows, that was where he preferred to lurk. He never came within arm's reach of me, which was preferable and yet somehow offensive.

For the next two days, he came to the library in the afternoons, but he stayed hunched and cast me furtive glances, seemingly ready at any moment for me to realize what he was and run screaming from the castle. As if I'd looked at him without really seeing him yet.

For my part, I found myself trying to get him to smile, but if he responded to any jokes I tried, it was only to duck away. He smiled at walls, but he would not smile at me.

"I'm not ashamed of you," I finally announced, snapping my book closed and setting it aside. "I'm not the one asking you to hide. You're hiding yourself."

"You're hiding too," he said.

Not for the first time, I hated his sharp observations. He cloaked himself with shadows and raised shoulders; I cloaked myself with plain linen and amusement.

So I tried to reach beyond the amusement to honesty—

—and the words I found were:

"I'm ashamed of Beauty."

The fire crawled inside me. I breathed carefully, trying not to stoke the flames.

Beast looked at me from the corner of the library, his yellow eyes bright in the shadows. "What happened?"

I would never understand how that rough, snarling voice could be so gentle.

But even so, I couldn't say it, couldn't relive it and make it real with words. Each one would fuel the monster inside me, and I had already burned enough.

I was ready to leave when he changed his question.

"If you could be someone other than Beauty, who would you be?"

"Orla Byrne." I struggled to find a whimsical smile. "From across the sea. A pirate queen."

"Daring," he observed, that same steady tone he'd used on a peasant with runaway potatoes.

My smile came a little easier. I sat straight in my armchair and threw myself wholeheartedly into the whimsy.

"When I was barely fifteen and scrawny as a pea pod, a pirate ship came to loot my village. I snuck aboard the vessel and defeated every man at one-on-one combat, claiming the ship as my own. Since then, I am undefeated in battle, aided by my great weapon, Ruiner, forged from fairy steel in a dragon's flame."

As I waved my hand, the castle's own sense of humor manifested in my palm in the shape of a child's wooden sword. I nearly choked in surprise, though the enchantments should have long ago ceased to astonish me.

"A fierce weapon," Beast agreed, steady as ever.

But there it was, that smile. Turned not on a wall but on me. The expression was unnatural on an animal face, pulling his upper lip back to reveal his fangs, more snarl than smile. But somehow it was all the more endearing for the ridiculousness.

It was whimsical, something not for this world.

I stood upon my chair, almost overbalancing as the stuffed leather rolled like the sea beneath me. Let it be sea. Let it all be real.

Brandishing my fierce weapon at the ceiling, I cried, "Challenge me, anyone who dares. The last thing you ever feel will be the sting of Ruiner's blade as it pierces your heart."

My family would have been appalled. Astra would have yanked me from the chair herself. But Beast uncurled from his corner and stepped forward. He had no elegance as he walked upright, almost as little balance as I possessed on the soft cushion.

And in his hand—

His own wooden sword.

Though he could hardly grip it as his five fingers were tipped in awkward claws.

Still he raised it.

"Ah, a challenger!" I pointed my blade at his heart, even though he was still halfway across the room. "State your name, knave."

This time he gave me a real snarl as mischief sparkled in his eyes. "Aye, Orla, I challenge. I am Andre Wolf. Ye killed my crew and sank my *Sea Witch,* and today I'll have my revenge." His growling voice was perfectly suited to the skulking pirate.

My jaw hung open.

I'd never heard him string so many words at once.

"Ha!" I pressed one foot to the arm of the chair, which served as the banister of my grand galleon. "Thieves and cut-throats, the lot of them, good for only a watery grave. Attempt your revenge if you dare, and I'll sink you just the same."

He took a gentle swing at me, which I blocked with ferocity. I did have limited skills in swords, thanks to a brief education from Rob before Mother discovered the lessons and forbade them.

"You'll have to do better than that, Andre!" I jumped to the ground.

Beast stared at me for a moment, wide-eyed, and then his smile was back. He took another swing, committed this time. He was at least seven feet tall, and I was barely five and a half, but his slouch brought him closer to my level, and his grip was clumsier than mine. I almost knocked the sword from his hand just by deflecting his swing.

"I slaved for years for that ship," he snarled.

"You mean you stole it, pirate."

"Aye, I stole it. But I *slaved* for that theft."

I laughed and took a light jab at his side. He stumbled out of the way, crashing into the table beside my chair. It overturned, legs flying into the air like an unbalanced toddler.

"Destroying my cannons now!" I cried, outraged. "I'll not stand for that!"

He deflected my overhand strike, then delivered one of his own, which I was a little slow to match. The wooden sword smacked me in the shoulder, and I let out a sound that was mostly laughter with a little pain.

"I'm sorry. Are you—" He started to lower his sword, and I grinned triumphantly.

"Lowering your defenses, just as I planned!"

I leapt onto the chair once again and delivered him a devastating shoulder smack in return, though I had to reach awkwardly for it. Based on his expression, the hit may as well have been the fluttering of a bird's wing. Not only that, but in my overreach, I stumbled. When I tried to catch myself, my foot slipped against the chair's arm and I toppled.

I let out a yelp, dropping my sword, flailing to catch myself before I hit the floor—

But Beast caught me first.

He'd dropped his own sword to catch me with both arms. He had to hunker to keep his balance, but he succeeded where I'd failed. I clung to his suit jacket with both hands as my mind tried to account for the hard landing that hadn't come.

He said my name twice before I looked up. His face was inches from mine, and much more terrifying up close, like staring into the waiting jaws of a predator.

But it was the vise of his arms around me that scared me most.

"Let me go," I panted, struggling. "Please. Let me go!"

He lifted me first, unhooking my foot where it was still tangled between the cushion and the arm of the chair, and in that moment of holding, that moment of delay, my panic doubled.

"Let me go!" I shrieked.

He set me down, and I bolted, pressing myself against a bookcase, gasping for breath.

He was apologizing, had been from the start, and the madness of it washed over me. He hadn't done anything wrong. He'd saved me from a fall. But I turned my face into a bookshelf and cried anyway.

Because I couldn't escape his arms unless he let me.

Because I was not an undefeated pirate queen at all, just a broken beauty.

"Beauty, I'm sorry." His voice was ragged at the edges. "I'm sorry I frightened you."

I wanted to tell him he hadn't, but he had. I wanted to say it didn't matter, but it did.

Mostly I wanted to run Stephan through with a real sword and know he was gone forever, that I would never see his gleaming eyes again or hear his voice say, *My Beauty.* Perhaps a sword of fairy steel could kill even his ghost, could cut the handprint from my soul and the shadow from my shoulder.

But I had no fairy sword, and that ghost was all I could feel.

It may have been the stress and worry that brought on my fever—if so, irony was a cruel master. Father took my siblings to a dinner party one evening, and I stayed home to recover, the lone member of the household.

Stephan heard I was sick.

Stephan came to the house, asked to see me.

I hadn't thought to tell any of the staff he was unwelcome. Even if I had thought of the idea, I would have restrained myself for fear of gossip reaching my family. Since I was sick in bed, the maid brought Stephan to my room, and he dismissed her before I had a chance to catch my bearings.

Then it was just the two of us, alone in my bedroom.

And I saw the gleam in his eyes.

"Stephan, don't," I begged.

But he had as little ear for my refusals as ever.

Even in the best of circumstances, I couldn't have hoped to fight him off. At least I could have tried. But I was weak and feverish. Caged in his heat.

And my world burned to ash.

"You'll always be mine," he whispered at the end, mouth pressed to my ear. "My Beauty."

The marriage was only a formality now; in his eyes, he already owned me.

And in my eyes, the worst outcome was not choosing between marriage and death, although I considered both. The worst outcome was trying to imagine how I could ever look in a mirror and see Beauty again.

News of Father's bankruptcy came the very next day, my saving grace, my mercy. My escape.

An escape I chased all the way into the arms of a beast.

I managed only one sentence through my tears: "Don't go."

I knew Beast would disappear if I didn't say it, vanish into thin air and go somewhere I couldn't follow and blame himself. I wanted to hide my sobs, but I would rather be seen than lose his company.

My fingernails dug into the bookshelf. I pressed my

forehead to my knuckles and stared at the leather book spines, though I could not see much through my tears. I imagined reading folktales and poetry and poetry and folktales until Stephan's touch faded from my skin. My breathing slowly evened, widening lengths between gasps, until it finally made way for the return of silence. My knees trembled.

"Can I help?" Beast asked, his voice small and faraway. He'd retreated to his shadowed corner.

I closed my eyes and filled my lungs.

"Did anyone else have a room in the castle before me?" My voice rasped from a raw throat.

"Once," he admitted.

Truth. Here I was, seeking it again. I didn't want to know. But I had to know. Truth was the thornbush on the path, and unless I pressed my way through it, I could never move forward again.

"Was she like me?" I turned enough to see him, though I kept my shoulder curled into the bookcase as if I could draw it around me like a blanket.

He was hunched in the corner, crouched low to the ground without sitting.

"No one is like you," he said.

No, I didn't think so either. No one could be this shattered and remain standing. Maybe I was the ghost.

"She saw me on her first day here. She was here only one day."

Like putting a hand to a hot coal. He'd been burned once, and when I came, he'd refused to make the same mistake.

I recognized that kind of hesitation, that kind of scar.

"Ask me," I said. "The question you have to ask."

He flinched.

"Ask me."

Without raising his eyes, he said, "Will you marry me, Beauty?"

I felt Stephan's skin, saw Stephan's eyes. I buried my arms to the elbows in the thornbush—

And I pushed a step forward.

"I can't," I said calmly, carefully, prevented from collapse only by the bookshelf beside me.

He looked at me, and I couldn't read his expression. Mine was likely just as strange.

"I lived in a different castle once." I swallowed. "And I gave a man a room. But when I wouldn't give him anything else, he took the castle by force. And then I had nothing left to give."

"Beauty." The way Beast said my name in that moment was the most painful thing I'd ever heard. The secret I'd kept from my sisters, from my father, from Rob—I'd told it to a stranger.

Three times, Stephan asked me to marry him. Three times, I said no. After that he didn't ask.

Three times, Beast asked me to marry him. Three times, I said no.

I waited to see what would come next.

He stayed in his corner, reached for me only with his gaze, but those yellow eyes pierced me to my soul.

"I promised you no harm," he said. "From me, from anyone. You're safe here."

His words renewed my tears, but this was not the wracking sobs of before; instead, it was a gentle mourning that I hadn't met him first. He would have liked the original Beauty, I thought. The confident, sharp-minded girl I'd been before my foundations cracked.

"Thank you," I choked out. "You are the most decent man I've ever met. I've seen a true beast."

If I could transfer the curse, I would. But all I had power to do was remove it, and I couldn't bring myself to do that. Not when lifting the curse was certain to change him, and I couldn't bear the uncertainty of change, of discovering him to be different than I'd imagined but only after I'd bound my life to his.

I wiped my tears and looked away. "You fought bravely, Andre. You have revenged your crew."

His measured silence between responses was a little less measured now.

"Then perhaps," he said, "my queen will grant a reward."

"Treasure?"

"A place in her crew."

At first, I stiffened, but his voice was light, and he didn't propose. We were once more in whimsy.

So I said, "Very well, Andre. I could use a cabin boy."

He snorted. "Very gracious, Your Majesty."

"Indeed. Now swab the deck."

I'd pushed my first few inches through the thorns, and though my arms bled, the pain of truth was not the burning agony of trauma. This fire was a cleansing one, the cauterizing of a wound rather than the extending of it, and although I breathed the ache, for the first time, I did not breathe the smoke.

CHAPTER 11

Where Beast had once been near impossible to find around the castle, now he seemed to be everywhere I looked. If I was not in my bedroom, Beast was nearby. I found I not only didn't mind but looked forward to the company.

The only time he did not accompany me was when I rode Honey, since he could not ride a horse himself. I rode Honey less and less often as the days went by.

On the rare occasions he was absent, I sought an audience in the throne room, and the doors opened to admit me. Together, we constructed the epic conflict of the peasants and the potatoes, which was eventually decided by cavalry attack, since peasants are notoriously weak against cavalry and potatoes are famously steady riders.

In the library, I played the violin for him, and we took turns reading. Now that he would let me see him, we could sit together at a desk, and I could correct his letters and pronunciation properly. He was not embarrassed by my coaching, and with gentle instruction, his reading skill increased quickly. He had a dedicated mind and did not abandon a task because it was difficult.

"If I am Whimsy," I told him once, "you are Fortitude."

He said, "Before long, we'll have too many names to keep straight."

"I can't imagine what you mean, Andre. Now where is Beast?"

I called him Andre sometimes, cherishing the reminder of that afternoon when I'd rediscovered hope. I had gathered the wooden play swords, afraid they would disappear if I didn't. His I kept in the chest at the end of my bed, but mine I wore belted around my waist. What a ridiculous image I would have made for society—a woman of age wearing a man's belt and a child's toy. But society could not reach its meddling fingers here. Not to our enchanted castle. And when I wore the sword, at times, Beast called me Orla, as if he cherished that afternoon the way I did.

Beast never pressured me for more truth, and he carefully kept his distance even when we shared a writing desk. It was a kind gesture, and I should have been relieved, but I found myself confused, because at times, I wished he would offer me his arm or sit closer at the desk rather than keeping a world of space between us. But I was also afraid if I told him as much, he would offer his arm and I would discover I couldn't take it without panic. If I was a mess of confusion, better to keep it to myself.

But there was one thing I could not remain silent about.

Whatever enchantment was on Beast was a cruel one. It obviously pushed him to ask his question whether he wanted to or not. Now that I could see his struggle, my heart softened. He did not want to marry me, just as I did not want to marry him. If I couldn't set him free, there was at least one thing I could give him.

"Whenever it pulls at you," I said, "ask."

For a while, he resisted, but eventually, he seemed to trust I was sincere. Besides, if it began to pull at him in earnest, the only way to resist was to avoid me entirely, and neither of us wanted that.

So he began to ask every evening: "Beauty, will you marry me?"

It was strange at first, an abrupt outburst in conversation, to which I would say, "I can't," and we would haltingly resume whatever we had been discussing before. But with each asking and each refusal, my anxiety eased by degrees until the question no longer brought me panic or unwelcome reminders. It became as normal as a remark on the weather:

"Is it always spring here?"

"Yes. The seasons exist only beyond the gate."

"Better to see the flowers bloom, I suppose."

"Will you marry me, Beauty?"

"Not today."

"I don't mind the flowers, but I miss the snow."

Sometimes after we moved on, we would both laugh at the absurdity of our situation, an enchanted boy and a runaway girl in a magic castle dancing around the topic of marriage.

As I grew more comfortable, my answers changed. Sometimes it was, "Not today." Sometimes it was, "And sacrifice my lifelong dream of being an old, unmarried crone shaking my cane at interloping children? Goodness, no."

Once, it was, "I am much too old for you, wee beastie."

"Oh, indeed?" His mouth was already tugging at a smile.

"Oh, indeed. I may not look it, but when I was eighteen, I went on a daring quest to the fountain of youth. Now I am eternally as you see before you, but my soul is hunched with a thousand years of age."

"A thousand years. Incredible. Tell me how the world has changed."

"The invention of people was quite bizarre."

He hacked and choked; he must have been swallowing when I made him laugh. Another of his many human traits.

"You are a person," he pointed out.

"I suppose I am, wee beastie. You must forgive me; my mind is befuddled by age."

"I'd best find a cane, so you can shake it at interlopers and fulfil your lifelong dream."

He always remembered details like that. Things I said on a whim, he gathered and tucked carefully away to recall at a later time. It was endearing to be so well heard, but it was also frightening, for my tongue was not a bridled one, and I said plenty of things I wished we could both later forget.

Such as the night he asked if I would marry him and I said, "You would do better to marry Astra."

"Oh?" He had no eyebrows, but the ridges above his yellow eyes often took the part, the fur rising and scrunching as it would on a human face.

"She is of age, beautiful, versed on all the foremost topics of society."

"I suppose men have married for less."

Even though I'd introduced the topic, my chest tightened, and I wished I hadn't spoken, hadn't given myself the image of Astra in the castle instead of me. I could not imagine her actually saying yes, but she was twenty-five and desperate. She could have her heart's desire in gems and wealth from the castle, and magic itself was priceless. With her knowledge, she could certainly leverage a marriage to Beast to her own advantage, especially after the enchantment was lifted and he became a man again.

She would order him around, and he would accommodate her because he was kind and had a sense of honor and duty. Perhaps he would even love her for setting him free. Perhaps they would both be unspeakably happy, having gained everything they ever wanted.

If I was kind, I would have gone home and spoken to Astra, arranged things myself, if not for my sister's sake, at least for the sake of my friend. But I did not feel kind.

"Beauty?" Beast tilted his head, studying me.

I looked away. "You must resent me."

"No, why would I ever?"

"Because all it would take to save you would be a simple yes. And every night, I say no."

"I don't begrudge your choices."

Of course he said that, because he was kind. If Astra had been at the castle, he would have been free already.

"You've done so much for me, and I've done nothing for you."

He stared at me, and the silence stretched. He couldn't deny the truth.

"You listen when I speak," he finally said. "And when I read. You are everything, Beauty."

But I couldn't believe it, not when he'd welcomed a girl to his castle to lift the enchantment and all I had done was use it and him for my own purposes.

"As long as I'm here," I said, "you'll always be a beast. Never a man."

"If you need me to be a beast," he insisted, "then I'll be a beast."

But that only made everything so much worse.

"I'm taking Honey for a ride."

I left the castle with hurried steps, and he didn't follow.

The wind stung my face as we galloped. Though I rarely let my eyes wander out to the forest, I looked to the trees that led toward my family's cottage. My eyes widened, and I pulled Honey to a halt. She stamped and danced a few steps to the side, perhaps as uneasy as I was about the sight.

The treetops roiled as if they hid a hurricane, every branch whipping in a different direction. The sky above the castle was as clear as ever, but when I squinted at the horizon, I could swear I saw storm clouds flicker.

Heart pounding, I glanced back at the castle. Then at the gate.

Honey whinnied, and I leaned forward to rub her neck.

While I waited in indecision, the storm slowly calmed. The churning treetops slowed until, at last, all was still.

When I returned to the castle, I asked Beast about the forest.

"It only abides an intruder for so long," he said, looking uneasy. "A storm like that means someone wandered too far in."

I realized the meaning underneath his words. "Can you not enter the forest?"

"No. The trees come alive to keep me out."

I knew he was cursed to be a beast, knew he needed a marriage agreement to escape. But I hadn't realized he was a prisoner of the castle on top of it all. I thought of him in the throne room, learning military strategy from a silent instructor. Even knowing he had no taste for it, I'd never asked if he could leave. The castle had never locked me in a room, so in my arrogance, I'd imagined he possessed the same freedoms.

The duties of a prince, he'd told me.

Every day, the truth grew thornier.

I bit my tongue.

Then the rest of the message sank in.

"My family," I asked. "Are they in danger from the forest?"

His yellow eyes mourned. "If they dive too deep."

Astra would never come after me, nor would Callista.

But Rob might. Or Papa.

"My father came to the castle once," I said.

"I can't speak for the whims of the enchantments."

"Some prince you are." Once again, it was unfair of me. Hadn't I just realized he was a prisoner?

That night, I closed myself in my bedroom and sat at the window, watching the forest. All was still.

But in the silence of my thoughts, I realized—

There was someone else who would come after me. If he only knew where I was.

CHAPTER 12

Where Stephan's ghost had been temporarily banished, now it lurked in every shadow again. I expected that, at any moment, the castle doors would swing open to admit him, and when I turned, I would see his gleaming eyes.

Even music could not calm me because my fingers clenched the notes and the bow held all the weight of my anxiety.

"Beauty, what's wrong?" Beast asked. He had his own armchair now, next to mine, but with distance enough that he couldn't reach me.

I did not uncurl from my violin. Instead, I mumbled into its side, "Read me a story?"

He turned to our favorite book of folklore, and as he read the story of the three undefeated princes and the wily plough boy who tricked them in their own arena, I tuned out the details, listening only to the rumbling growl of his voice. It was music enough.

"Royalty is always foolish in these stories," he observed.

"Because these are stories for the common man." I sighed, unable to lift my head. "And we are envious."

Had he been envious when he made his wish? Had he traveled the world to find a fairy only to have it trick him into becoming prince of an empty castle?

I did not even know where he called home.

"Before Andre Wolf was a pirate and a cabin boy . . ." I swallowed. "Who was he?"

Beast gathered his thoughts in silence, and I felt no urge to rush him. He would speak when ready; he always did.

"He was born by a river," he said at last, "that led to the sea."

I asked no questions, just listened. Andre was the son of a fisherman, his father a good man who provided for his family until an ambitious voyage and a late-season storm ended his life. I thought of my own father's lost fortune and the men who had drowned along with it. Ours was not the only family to have been ruined. Andre's mother, a strong woman by the name of Henriette, provided for the family in whatever way she could.

With every word, my chest ached. We were shoulder-deep in truth, and I felt the thorns.

Andre's only sibling was his older brother, Bastien, who should have been the rock of the family. Instead, he was as unsatisfied as the tides, imagining there was a fortune to be had in this venture or that. Each foundation his mother worked so hard to secure, he overturned in a gamble until she could bear it no longer, and after an exchange of harsh words, her eldest left home for good. If he ever found his desired fortune, he never sent word or brought it home.

In Bastien's shadow, I saw Astra.

Beast fell silent until I asked, "How old were . . . was Andre?"

"Twelve when Bastien left. Close to sixteen when he followed."

"How old when he faced Orla the pirate queen?"

"Nineteen."

I raised my head. Judging by maturity alone, I would have guessed him Stephan's senior. But Stephan was Callista's equal in age. Andre was only a year advanced from me.

I smiled.

"I'm eighteen."

"Ah"—his nose twitched—"the age at which you seek the fountain of youth. It's a big year for you."

It was indeed.

"Did my cabin boy seek a fountain of youth when he left home?"

Beast looked away. "Of a sort."

I almost spoke again but caught my tongue, pressed it against my front teeth. Silence was as important as speech during our conversations. Beast would not compete with me to speak. If he had more to say, it would remain unsaid if I spoke first, and I never wanted a single one of his rare, fascinating words to go unheard.

A log in the fire popped. I willed it to hush.

"He imagined . . ." Beast paused, darted a glance at me, then away again. "He imagined himself better than his brother. But he chased the same selfish dreams."

How many times had I counted myself Astra's superior?

Still, he was kinder than I. "I don't believe that, Andre."

His yellow eyes met mine.

"You revenged your crew at the risk of your life and with

nothing to gain. Given choice, yours is not a heart that stays away from home."

Whether it was to ease the burden on his mother or to chase his wayward brother, he must have felt he had no choice but to leave.

"Is yours?" he asked.

The log snapped, collapsing into the fire with a burst of sparks. I jumped.

"My family is fine," I said, though it did not answer his question.

"Do you miss them?"

Something inside twisted, a silent cry, but I said, "No."

He waited, and the pressure built.

I stood, my bare feet sinking in the fur rug. The spines of every book looked the same to me, but I grabbed one off the shelf anyway and flipped through it.

The pages were blank.

"Is this your doing?" I looked up at him with a narrow glare.

He only waited.

"My family would not want me home," I said at last. "Not if they knew."

"Why not?" he asked softly.

He had to know why not. It was obvious.

"My father would have to either marry me off or risk defending me at the cost of his own reputation." I tried to keep my voice breezy, as if I were speaking of someone else, the way Beast had told me his own story under a different name. "My brother would say, 'I warned you,' because he did indeed warn me. My sister . . ."

I thought of the spiteful kiss, of Astra's firsthand witness.

"My sister would say I walked myself in," I said. "And she would be right."

Beast was silent. I felt my hands trembling, but when I looked, they were still as death.

"Bring me that book?"

I looked up in surprise. Beast was not one to suddenly change the topic or avoid a subject, but perhaps I'd made him uncomfortable. My cheeks heated.

I stepped forward to give him the volume, but when I extended it, his clawed hand did not lift.

He said, "I don't want it after all."

Now my hands trembled.

"If you did walk in," he said, "it's no obligation to stay."

Don't look at me like that. His gaze was painfully heavy, even more painfully tender.

"Even if you gave him a room," he said, "it gave him no right to the castle."

Please.

It had the melody of logic, but the dark corners of my mind did not want to hear music. I curled in my chair again, wrapped around my silent violin. Beast said nothing else, but he stayed with me in the dark.

I sought out the fairy. She danced to the fence, stood before my chest, her eyes level with mine. She had emotionless, solid blue eyes, but she smiled like a human.

"Are you ready to make a wish?" She cocked her head, blue hair floating around her as if suspended in water.

"I'm considering. Tell me first—can you make me forget?"

"Make a wish, and you will see what is possible."

It was no wonder even a wise Wolf could fall victim when there was no way to test the ground.

Suppose I forgot only to meet him at some future day. He would have every advantage. And without knowing why I stayed, I would leave the safety of the castle. It was foolish to even consider.

But suppose I wished to go back in time. Would that claim my memories as well? Suppose I'd already wished it, and without knowledge of what was to come, every mistake and every pit of spikes had ensnared me just the same. Perhaps this was the fifth time I'd stood before the fairy and wished to turn the sun back to a day before Stephan.

"Why did you turn Andre into a beast? What was his wish?"

She only smiled. "Do you wish to know?"

"Do you enjoy toying with people?"

"I only grant wishes. What you wish for is yours."

"I'm sure he didn't wish to be a beast."

"Did he not?" She reached out to touch the fence post, and the gold gleamed brighter at her hand. "Beauty, of all people, knows the weight in a word. Be ever so careful of the words in a wish."

"Can I free him?" I swallowed. "Can I free him with a wish?"

I thought she would tell me to wish and see.

But it was worse.

"No wish may be undone by another. Only by—"

"Completion. I remember."

Completion of what? Of the wish? Of regret? Beast had some kind of out through a marriage agreement, a cruel corner.

"Something other than marriage," I said. "Please. Anything."

"To each wish is its completion, and no other may do."

I smacked my palm into the fence post, shaking the fairy loose. She stepped back.

"It isn't fair!" I shouted. "He made a wish, but it takes someone else to get him out? It isn't fair to him."

If no one said yes, he would live in that lonely castle forever. The kindest heart in humanity would be lost.

"No one lives isolated," the fairy said, unmoved. "Existence is a chord, every life a note. Wishers and granters and all between. Will you now wish?"

If I couldn't help Beast with a wish, I could at least help my family. Reverse their fortunes.

But he'd warned me not to.

"Has anyone ever wished," I asked, "without regret?"

She smiled.

And that was answer enough.

The castle was packed to the rafters with magic. Since arriving, I had been submerged daily, from books that shelved themselves to the ever-blooming gardens. I could not deny the ease of life as I drifted in such a current, could not deny that my eyes still grew wide with wonder or that I did not profit off the unearned riches—my horse, my violin, the sword at my waist.

But I recognized the emptiness too. Anything broken in the castle repaired itself. Anything summoned eventually vanished. Even the books in the library could one day easily be void of words.

Nothing was real.

And I knew the fountain of magic would not quench my thirst.

CHAPTER 13

I lay on my bed that night, staring at the moonlit window.

Beast was not ill-mannered, though he possessed none of the manners of society, and there was no tact in his honesty, which revealed it so plainly as honesty. Since my first step into the castle, he'd been only kind to me.

Stephan had been charming at first, but no one would call him kind. He was always eager to speak ill of someone. I hadn't noticed only because the people he spoke ill of were ill people. And I had enjoyed trading secret laughs with him behind my own sister's back.

Beast had never made a careless comment, even when I gave him opportunity to. Instead, he said, *Whimsy is welcome here*, and if I was selfish, he was too.

I couldn't offer a wish. I couldn't agree to marriage.

But there had to be something I could do.

The dark hours passed until, at last, I rose from bed. A candle on my desk lit itself, and I seated myself in the chair.

"I'm coming to you instead of a fairy," I told the castle. "Don't disappoint me now."

It was empty magic, sure, but empty magic had its place. It

couldn't quench a deep thirst, but it could create an environment to do so. My wooden sword was proof of that.

I was no artist, but I let a quill guide my imagination. The castle had never needed more than my thoughts.

And outside my window, I was sure a dream took shape.

The next morning, I left my sword in the chest with Beast's and my shawl with it. I wanted to be unburdened for the adventure ahead.

When I exited my bedroom, Beast was already waiting in the hallway, curled beside my door. He scrambled to his feet when I appeared, and I'd never seen such a light of excitement in his eyes.

"Was it you?" he asked.

"Was what me?" I meant to feign innocence, but the corners of my mouth betrayed me. I cleared my throat. "I'm told there's a festival in town—can you imagine?"

"No." He smiled. "I've never been to one."

I'd thought as much if he came from a remote fishing village.

"Then we'd best visit."

I held my breath, waiting, but he didn't offer me his arm. Instead, he gestured for me to take the stairs ahead of him, and that was alright too.

The castle doors opened ahead of us, and the spring air brought the sound of festival music, cheerful lutes and flutes that heralded fun to be had. The field beyond the gardens was filled with rows of colorful tents, a sight to rival the flower beds around us. Though it was a finer setup than I'd ever seen, I felt my childhood in a rush of lightness.

"Race you." I touched the beast's arm as I passed, caught a flash of his bright eyes in my glance.

Each step carried the shining world and the memories closer.

So many events in our port city had brought a fair to the streets—St. Ifan's day, the harvest feast—and I relished each one. There was no better home to whimsy than a festival. One year, Rob took a prize in archery, and his hug lifted me clean off the ground. Even Astra's usual impatience softened at a festival, enough to include me as she and Callista flitted from the perfume stall to the wood carvings to the display of rings fine enough to grace the hand of a queen. We laughed together—*There, Astra, a ruby to match your complexion. Callista, a lily perfume, your favorite! Oh, Beauty, see the instruments!*

I burst through the line of tents, and I circled in wonder. The scent of pies and ale carried from one vendor, the aroma of roasting meat from another. The lively music brightened the air. One tent had a collection of furs, another held happy songbirds in gilded cages. There were spices, foreign fruits, rugs, jewelry, even a collection of clucking chickens.

And not a soul besides us.

Beast approached slowly, shoulders hunched, his wide eyes taking each sight in carefully, like it might disappear.

It would. But not yet.

"Alright, Andre"—his eyes swung to mine, and I spread my arms wide—"where to first?"

He darted a look in every direction, and he appeared so

lost, it plucked my heart. I hesitated, then reached out to grasp his hand. And then we stared at each other, his palm warm against my fingers, the softness of fur strange beneath my thumb, until I tugged him forward to the first tent, and then I pointed at each rug as if it were a wonder, as if his castle weren't full of them, and somewhere along the way, he curled his long fingers gently against mine, so gently that I felt the cold of his claws without a prick.

I pulled him from tent to tent, and invisible vendors raised wares for our consideration while a lute bobbed in and out of our path. I reached out once to pluck its strings, and it offered itself to me.

"Do you play all instruments?" Beast asked, with so much faith in his voice, I couldn't resist.

With full confidence, I strummed a discordant note. The lute shuddered in my hands.

"If I had a bow," I said.

"If you had a bow," Beast agreed.

We laughed as the lute bobbed away.

We visited the food stalls, and although Beast declined each offering, I did not. I bit into a pear that dripped sweet trickles down my chin.

"This is where a juggler would perform," I told him, gesturing to the empty places between tents. "And here a stilt walker. You are tall enough to fill the part. Imagine how you would tower if we raised you on wooden planks."

He wrinkled his nose at the concept. With his unsteady balance, I couldn't blame him.

"Then a juggler you must be."

Two leather balls appeared for me. I tossed both in the air and managed to catch one though the other hit the grass.

"Strange game," Beast said.

"The point is to keep both aloft, but alas, my skill extends only to instruments. A fearless cabin boy may have a better chance."

I handed the juggling balls to him. His fingers gripped them awkwardly, and he stared more awkwardly still.

I laughed. "Just try. You saw my attempt."

He tossed both at once and caught neither, but I applauded anyway.

"The most spectacular juggling I have ever seen!" I waved an arm behind me at the empty tents. "And no witness to contradict!"

He gave a little snarl in my direction, but his eyes remained bright.

At the end of the line of tents was a wooden platform. I leapt up the three steps and shouted from its center, "Upon this stage, a play! The great battles of men and angels, the miracles of God, enacted for your entertainment and edification!"

Father had always enjoyed the plays most.

"Which shall it be, wee beastie? *The Great Flood*? Perhaps *The Prophet Among Lions*?"

"I'm unfamiliar with either," Beast admitted.

I lowered myself to the edge of the stage, dangling my legs above the grass. "Did you never hear the priests read scripture at church?"

"We had no church."

How Father would have wept to hear it.

"Do you believe in God, then?"

"Honestly, I'm not sure what such a thing means."

I was the worst to explain it. I did not know my own beliefs.

"Creation. Heaven and hell." I grasped unsuccessfully, my cheeks growing hotter. Father would have been ashamed. "Life after death."

Beast considered. I restrained myself from dumping more unclarity.

"Life after death sounds like a second chance," he said quietly. "I'd like to believe in that."

It stilled my thumping heart.

"Me too," I whispered.

"Will you marry me, Beauty?"

"Alas!" I heaved a sigh. "I am far too busy. There's a festival in town, you know. Perhaps you could ask again tomorrow."

"Rest assured, I will."

We laughed again. As I braced myself to jump from the stage, Beast offered me a hand.

I took it and jumped.

"Did I hurt you?" he asked.

I looked at my hand. There was a thin, white scratch at the base of my pointer finger, but I hadn't felt it. He was so fearful to cause pain in even the small things.

"You would never hurt me," I said, curling my fingers. "Come, we'll miss the archery tournament!"

We wasted our day at an imaginary festival, lost in whimsy. The impressive Sir Charles bested me in archery. My single shot did not even make contact with the target, which was the closest to gold anyone could hope to come except for Sir Charles, who improved my shot by a mere inch.

Sir Charles also took the prize in jousting, which Beast and I declined to participate in because I lacked a sufficient coat of arms and he was the presiding royalty, obligated to serve as an unbiased judge.

By the end of the day, Beast grew hungry enough to eat a leg of lamb, though he was still so shy that he made me agree to look away. I sampled almost every snack the enchantments had to offer, but nothing impressed me more than the pear. I returned for two more before the sun began to set.

As the light faded, the tents rolled their walls and toppled their poles. The wares faded until, at last, it was only an empty field.

"I miss it already," Beast said.

"Then you have truly been to a festival."

"Thank you."

My ears flamed. I started to tell him it was a matter of no consequence, but I couldn't. It was certainly of consequence to me.

Something bothered my nose. In the absence of festival foods, a murky scent weighted the air. I turned toward the forest, and in the last remaining light, I saw a mass of gray above the treetops.

"Fire," Beast said quietly, his gaze in the same direction as mine.

My stomach clenched.

Was it Stephan, burning a forest to reach me?

Or was my family in danger?

We watched without words as the smoke climbed higher.

The festival music was fresh on my mind, and with it, all the merry memories I'd forgotten existed. My chest ached for an evening at home in a cramped cottage, shoulder to shoulder with my family. If it wasn't too late. If they hadn't forgotten me. If they weren't lost.

I looked at Beast. His eyes were already on me.

"I understand," he whispered.

How did he know the things I didn't even speak?

"I can't hide forever," I said.

"No," he agreed, looking away. "A heart like yours has to know."

The darkness deepened around us. Every castle window spilled welcoming light, beckoning me back to my safety, my escape. But if I turned away now, I would never turn back.

"The woods aren't safe," Beast said.

He took my hand and pressed a gold ring into my palm. It matched the ring that had first brought me to the castle.

"Turn it three times to be home." He closed my fingers over it. His hand lingered.

"The same to return?" I asked.

"Should you wish to return."

"Of course!" I swallowed. "Of course."

But he wouldn't meet my eyes. He lowered his hand, stepped back.

With nothing else to do, I slid the ring onto my thumb. It was heavier than I expected. I bit my lip.

"You're captain while I'm gone, Andre."

I could hardly see him in the dark now, just a looming shadow almost out of arm's reach.

"I'll try not to sink it," he said, but there was no amusement in his voice. Only the same weight I felt on my hand.

I pinched the ring between my thumb and pointer finger, but then I froze.

My first instinct was not to turn it but to remove it. My escape had never been safer, never been more comfortable. I couldn't leave.

But that was just it, wasn't it? All that selfishness. If I didn't find my way out, I would drown in it, and I would take Beast with me.

"Beauty"—his voice cracked—"will you marry me?"

My breath caught.

He'd never asked twice in a day before.

Perhaps the enchantment pressed him harder because I was leaving.

"I can't." My old response. I could not bring myself to add whimsy this time.

I gripped the ring.

And I turned it three times.

CHAPTER 14

The cottage seemed smaller than I remembered. I could have tucked it into one corner of a ballroom in the castle and forgotten it was ever there. The single front window spilled firelight across a flower garden along the front edge of the house. Seeing the line of rose bushes, I almost turned the ring again, almost turned back. Perhaps I might have if not for Rob's hollering voice.

"Beauty! It's Beauty!"

I turned to find him running at me from the woodshed like Honey at a gallop, and I barely had a moment to prepare myself before he swept me right off my feet in a hug. I clung to him harder than I thought possible, all the festival memories twice as fierce and carried aloft in a flood of other forgotten things.

"Beauty, I thought you were dead! I thought—"

He was crying—Rob, who never cried except for severe injury and love.

"I'm alright," I choked out. I'd made him worry all this

time. I hadn't even said goodbye the night I'd left. "Rob, I'm so sorry."

After he'd finished crushing my ribs, he dragged me inside to the rest of the family. They'd heard a commotion, so Father was already at the door as we burst in, and then his eyes widened and his face paled like I was a plague victim up from my grave. He wrapped me in a hug as well, and while I was still in his arms, Callista gave a shriek and latched on too.

Had the drafty cottage always been so warm?

"Astra!" Rob called out. "Beauty's home!"

I pulled away enough to see Astra standing between the small kitchen and the smaller front room.

"I told you she was fine," Astra said. "Beauty is always fine."

She did not smile, but I chose to believe she was pleased in her own way at the news.

Father drew me to a chair by the fire and bundled me in blankets. I realized it was winter for them, that in the rush of family, I hadn't even seen the world frosted white. Callista kept patting my arms and shoulders while I tried to brush her away.

"I thought the monster ate you," she said. "We all did."

For a moment, I couldn't understand what monster she referred to.

Then I thought of Beast, of his snarling smile and his awkward claws gingerly curled around a book.

"He's not a monster," I said.

"Foolish girl," Father murmured, stroking my hair as he would when I was a child. "Going in my place. Foolish girl."

"What's happened?" Rob crouched beside me, gripping the

arm of the chair while I kept my hands clasped in my lap. "Tell us everything since you left."

There was so much to tell. It was a lifetime since I'd last been in this room with them. Since then, I'd been Orla Byrne, the pirate queen. And an explorer who found the fountain of youth. I felt that thousand years of age on my shoulders now.

"You first," I managed.

Rob worked with a moneylender in town, helping keep books and collect payments. He and Father still managed our bit of land, and they did it well. Callista was engaged to a boy who lived a mile down the road.

Callista. Not Astra. Even as Callista announced the engagement, she looked down as if embarrassed, a flush in her cheeks. I hoped it was at least partly from happiness.

"The men here are all poor as an empty flour sack." Astra sniffed. "It's a sad woman who would settle."

Rob grunted. "I'm a man here, Astra."

"Yes, and no woman will settle for you, will she?"

"Tell us now, Beauty," Father insisted. "Are you home to stay? How did you escape? Should we be ready for an attack?"

He said it so calmly, as if fully prepared to fight off a seven-foot beast and the entire enchanted forest if need be.

"I'm not a prisoner, Father." I swallowed. "In truth, he's very kind."

They all stared at me as if I'd grown extra limbs with the statement.

"And here I thought you brought his severed head in that box," Astra drawled. "Or some story like that."

I looked down at my feet and frowned to see a box there.

With the gold trim, it certainly didn't belong to the cottage. I lifted it gingerly to my lap. Knowing the castle, it might have packed up the entire festival and sent it with me, ready to spring out of the box and overtake our land with tents.

But when I peeked inside, I understood.

"I brought gifts." As if it had been my intention all along.

First was a gown obviously meant for Astra, a shimmering silver to complement her auburn hair, the trailing sleeves so thin, they were almost gossamer. Small jewels patterned the bodice, and the skirts carried white embroidery so fine, even she couldn't have matched it. My wardrobe must surely have been thrilled to finally have a willing recipient for its contents.

But to my surprise, Astra turned her head. "I don't want it."

"Of course you want it!" Callista scoffed and gathered the gown in her arms, tossing it to Astra. Despite Astra's words, she didn't let the fine material touch the floor.

The gown had been too large to fit in the box, but I was hardly surprised and certain there were more gifts to come.

Sure enough, in a blink, there was a candle in an ornate silver holder with a curved handle. I felt it was meant for Callista, but a candle seemed paltry after Astra's gown. Nevertheless, I handed it to her with false confidence.

She frowned over it as well, though I could see her gathering gratitude anyway. But as she touched the wick almost curiously, the candle lit itself.

She gasped, dropping it. The candle did not separate from the holder, nor did the flame blow out or burn the floor. When she hesitantly lifted it again, tilting it this way and that, she broke into a delighted grin.

"It doesn't melt the wax!"

"You could sell an enchanted candle for a fortune," Astra said.

"Never!" Callista said fiercely, and I knew it was not for my sake she said it.

Next came a book for Father. The tremble in his jaw and the reverence with which he turned the pages told me it was scripture.

"How . . . ?" He swallowed, staring at me in wonder.

I only hoped it would never disappear.

He rested his hand on my head again.

I looked up at Rob, then down at the empty box. The seconds passed, but nothing appeared.

"The best gift is having you home," he said graciously.

Then I heard a whinny from the front yard and set the box aside.

"Come with me."

Callista lent us her candle, and Rob followed me into the yard where Honey was waiting, in full tack. As soon as I saw her, I knew it was only right.

"I didn't even see your horse earlier," Rob said, looking around desperately like a stable might pop up at any moment. "We don't have anywhere to keep her."

"She's your horse, Rob." I smiled. "Her name is Honey."

Hearing her name, Honey trotted forward and gave Rob a solid headbutt greeting. He laughed, rubbing first his forehead, then hers. She shook her mane.

"And I'm sure if you look behind the house," I added, "there will be somewhere to keep her."

The castle was not one for oversights. It learned such thoughtful attention to detail from its master.

Sure enough, it wasn't quite a stable, but there was a horse shed already filled with hay, just the size for Honey.

Rob led the mare into the single stall, stroking her neck in wonder.

"Enchantments." He seemed unsure if it was a question or a comment.

I only shrugged.

"The castle is . . . incredible," I said. "Tea pours itself. Food appears. My wardrobe offers me dresses whether I want them or not."

"I noticed you're still plain for all this extravagance."

"You know me." I shook my head. "I never cared for ribbons." And more than ever, I hated the heavy skirts. Better to be plain and familiar.

"You used to care a little." His voice had lowered, and his gaze was piercing. "But something changed—before the beast, the bankruptcy. Something happened."

I hadn't expected to be cornered so soon.

But I'd come here for truth, thorns and all.

I looked away, nodding. And I held my breath in the wait.

"But you look happy now," he said.

I glanced up in surprise. He smiled, and my shoulders eased.

"I am," I admitted.

And for a girl who didn't believe in miracles, such a thing came suspiciously close to being one.

"Then that's what matters."

Rob unsaddled and brushed Honey, her nosing him all the while, throwing off his balance whenever he found it. They were a good pair, and she would be a huge benefit for his work collecting debt payments around the city. The castle had provided the perfect gifts for my family while I was still too self-absorbed to think clearly.

"I missed you." My voice cracked.

Rob turned and gave me another hug, resting his head on mine. Then we went back inside to rejoin the family.

It was difficult to transition back to a straw mattress after sleeping on what could have passed for a cloud, but I made do. When I woke in the morning, I finally felt the cold, shivering as soon as I left the blankets. Before I remembered where I was, I looked for the breakfast tray, and I was already thinking of Beast.

Then I stopped, bare feet cold against the wooden floor, as I realized I wouldn't see Beast today at all. There would be no afternoon in the library, no rumbling sound of his voice.

I shivered, rubbing the gold ring on my thumb.

Then I forced myself to dress. Astra was still asleep, so I crept from the room and found Callista in the kitchen. Without a word, she put me to work helping with breakfast, though my hands were clumsy. My calluses had disappeared at the castle.

"Well, if I had any doubt you were being treated well"—Callista rolled her eyes—"it's gone now."

My ears burned.

She ordered me to knead dough, and only as I reached for it did I remember my ring. I hesitated, then worked it free and set it on the table. As I kneaded, I cast frequent glances at it, my heart thumping with each glance, until I finally finished and could return it to my hand. I clenched my fist around the metal, taking a deep breath like a diver surfacing after starting to drown.

I wasn't stranded. I was with my family.

But I clutched the ring all the more.

We ate breakfast as a family, and it seemed quieter than I remembered until I realized it was me—I'd always filled the silence with chatter. Everyone looked at me between bites, waiting for me to speak, but as the pressure built, my mind only grew blanker and blanker.

"You said you're not a prisoner," Rob finally prodded.

"And she's certainly not been put to work." Callista reached out and shook my wrist. "Look at her soft baby hands."

Rob asked, "So what have you been doing all this time?"

I pulled free, face hot.

"I—I read. Mostly." I lifted my bowl to hide my face. "Scholars and poetry. And . . . folktales."

"It sounds as though you have everything you ever wanted," Astra said, setting her spoon down delicately.

"Are you here to stay?" Father leaned forward, his eyes on my ring, which suddenly felt cold against my finger. "You never answered. If you're not a prisoner, you can stay."

My tongue froze once more. If I told him I could stay but didn't want to, he would be heartbroken. To hear his daughter would choose to live with a beast rather than stay beneath his roof would break any father's heart.

"I've promised to return," I finally whispered.

It was unfair to Beast, to make him the monster tearing me from my family once more, but I couldn't bear to hear them tell me all the reasons I shouldn't want to go.

But Callista burst out anyway, her voice loud in the silence. "You shouldn't have to live your life with a beast. Not when you could marry Stephan!"

My blood froze, and I nearly dropped my bowl.

"What do you mean?" I rasped.

"He came to the house a month ago, looking to marry you! He told us how you were secretly engaged—Beauty, you could have said so. He was even ready to fight the beast to bring you home." Her eyes narrowed across the table. "But Father sent him away."

My hand was around my thumb, ready to turn the ring, ready to run, but I swallowed hard at her final statement. I looked at my father.

With a sigh, Father stood. "We should speak privately."

Privacy was hard to find in such a small space, but we went to the back room that served as Father's bedroom.

I kept my hand tight around the ring. "Is it true Stephan came?"

"He had quite a story for me. He claimed my daughter was pregnant."

I'd never felt the winter cut so keenly through walls.

"Papa—" My voice strangled.

Your father would be ashamed, Stephan whispered. I felt him hot on my skin, and my knees buckled.

Father grasped my elbows and eased me into a seat. I couldn't read his eyes.

"Papa," I tried again, but my jaw trembled. The heat was in my eyes. I couldn't see, but I couldn't break his gaze.

Don't send me away, I begged.

Papa, listen, I begged.

I couldn't say a thing.

Father's voice was quiet. "He spun some long-winded nonsense about how you were so in love, you couldn't wait. Secret engagement, planned elopement—none of it like my Beauty. I trust it was no crime against you to send him packing."

My wordless gaping only grew stronger.

He gripped my shoulders. "You told me you didn't want to marry him, girl. I didn't forget that."

I launched myself into his arms, buried my face in his chest, clung to him and let my tears fall. Eventually, I managed to choke the whole story out between my sobs, and my father held me all the tighter.

"Is there a child?" he asked.

I shook my head.

"Even if there was, we would sort it out. We would sort it out. I would sooner feed myself to a monster than my baby girl."

I finally realized how much I'd hurt him when I'd left. "I'm sorry, Papa. I didn't even do it to save you. I just wanted to run, and I ran . . . I ran as far as I could. Papa, I even hoped . . . I even hoped the beast would eat me and I'd be done."

"Don't say that." His arms nearly crushed me, and his own tears dripped on my hair.

Perhaps I was too big for his lap, but I still fit in his arms, and I stayed there until the sobs eased, until the salt of my tears felt different, until they soothed instead of burned. Mixed with all the stagnant fear and loss, there was relief too. There were still ghosts in the corners, but for the moment, they felt wispy, as they should. They felt like something that might one day fade to barely a shadow.

In my father's acceptance, I found the safety I'd searched for.

CHAPTER 15

Settling at home was as easy as falling into a familiar bed. There was a groove already worn for me; I had only to embrace it. I tended the house, which allowed Callista more opportunity to finish sewing orders, and where I could, I helped Papa. Even with crops dormant, there was work to be done—chickens to tend and firewood to stack. The winter air stung my face and lungs with invigorating force. If I had risen from the grave in returning to my family, it was not as an emaciated skeleton but as a woman reborn.

And yet . . .

I wondered if he went to the library without me, if he sat in his red armchair, or perhaps in mine. If he read the story of the swan who wished to be human.

Returning home had filled a hollow in my heart, but there was one remaining.

And I could not fill both.

My breath clouded the raw air. The chickens squawked in protest at my presence, demanding to be fed, but my eyes were on the enchanted forest. I tossed a careless handful of grain in the snow, then stepped over the scuttling birds to exit the fence gate. The trees loomed above me, taller with every step, and between them, I spotted a glimpse of glittering blue.

By the time I reached the forest's edge, she was gone.

Hadn't I decided by now?

Hadn't I learned?

If I made the selfish wish to have both, perhaps Beast's new prison would be our cottage, which was already too cramped. Or perhaps my family would be trapped at the castle, Callista ripped from her fiancé, Rob from his opportunities of advancement, none of us happy though we had all magic at our disposal.

This was not the place for magic; it was the place for decisions.

And I could not decide.

That evening, while Callista and I cooked, she gushed about the upcoming winter festival.

"It will be in the Merrells' barn." Her dashing fiancé, whom I had yet to meet, was the Merrell family's youngest boy, just turned twenty-one. "Everyone will bring food, and there will be dancing. You must come, Beauty."

I shifted, pressing all my weight into the dough I kneaded so Callista wouldn't make fun of my weak hands again. "Hardly a festival in one barn. Will the stilt walker endanger the rafters?"

"Must you always mince my words? A celebration, then. Tell me you'll come."

"When is it?"

"The first day of the new year."

"How far is that?"

She heaved a sigh. "You don't even keep track of years anymore? It's in a week."

A week to the new year. That made six months away from home. Six months with Beast. It seemed both too short and too long. I had lived forever in the castle at the same time I'd barely stepped foot in it at all.

"Tell me you'll come," she repeated with force.

After six months away, a week at home was not too much to ask.

"I'll come."

She squealed and threw her arms around me, almost impaling me with the knife in her hand.

"Careful, Callista!"

"Sorry!" She pulled back, laughing, and returned to the potatoes and onion.

After I handed the bread off to Rob to turn in the coals, Callista and I finished the stew.

"I'm sorry," she said quietly, wiping her hands without looking at me.

"Just put the knife down next time."

"No, about . . ." She gathered a deep breath, clutched the pot. "Telling you not to love before Astra. I thought I was being a good sister, but now I know it's not something you choose."

I didn't envy her the day she'd made the announcement of her own marriage. It couldn't have been easy.

I tried to say I hadn't loved Stephan, but I only said, "I forgive you."

And as I followed her to the fireplace, my steps felt a bit lighter. Until she hung the pot and turned to ask—

"Are you staying to marry Stephan? I think you should, no matter what Father says."

Rob's eyes were on me too, before he reached carefully to flip the bread.

"I don't love Stephan," I managed at last.

Callista gave me a pinched look. "Beauty, I've seen the way—"

"If she doesn't love him," Rob interrupted, "that's that."

I waited for him to say he'd warned me, that he'd predicted things with Stephan would end badly.

But he didn't.

"You never liked Stephan," Callista huffed, glaring at Rob.

"No, I didn't. But I don't make Beauty's decisions. If it's her decision not to marry him, I'm all the happier." Rob looked up at me. "And if he tries to hound you otherwise, you just say the word. I'll send him off with more force than Father did."

This was a different type of regret. Just when I'd thought I experienced the full spectrum.

I didn't know. No, that wasn't it. I didn't trust. When Stephan told me my family would hate me, I believed it.

Because why shouldn't they feel the same way I did?

I smashed my tongue between my teeth, felt the pain to the back of my skull.

"I—I have to—" I waved a useless hand, already stumbling toward the door.

Rob called, "Hey, there's a storm—"

The frozen wind caught me in the face, stole my breath. I would check on Honey. That way, if they asked—

Something darkened the road. Even squinting, I couldn't see clearly against the snow flurries. The shadow seemed to split, and most of it pulled away, but a sliver remained, growing closer until I could finally make out a form.

"Astra?" I covered my face with my sleeve, coughing against the sharp air.

"Commanding the storms now, Beauty?" Unlike me, she was smart enough to wear furs, and I could barely see her face below her hood.

"Was that a carriage?"

Callista had told me Astra was no longer as reluctant to work, but she was sewing for a wealthy client indeed if they were willing to ferry her by carriage in a storm.

She ducked into the house, and since the cold had reached my bones and iced out the foolishness, I followed. Astra and Callista took up conversation, allowing me to slip into our bedroom to breathe. That was enough.

I looked at the ring on my thumb. Slowly, I turned it, feeling the smooth gold glide across my skin.

Once.

Twice.

Would I go only to come back?

I stopped.

At dinner, Callista announced my promise to stay through the celebration.

Astra frowned at me but said nothing. I could not tell her mind.

Rob was clearer. "If this beast is so kind, surely he'd allow you to remain with your family."

It was the problem with my story. I focused my attention on my stew.

But my brother wasn't done.

"What demands has he made of you exactly?" he pressed. "What could he possibly want from a peasant girl?"

I heard the suspicion in his tone and the sparks of waiting rage.

"Beast isn't like that," I said firmly.

"Even though he threatened Father?"

"No, he . . . he's prince of the castle, Rob. He has duties. Enforcing law. Punishing theft. He doesn't *want* to do them."

Callista frowned. "Are you certain you're not imagining this beast to be better than it is?"

"I've been accused of imagining a great many things over the years," I said heatedly.

She took the barb for what it was and lowered her eyes.

"I believe you," Astra said.

I blinked. "What?"

She shrugged. "If I were in a castle full of enchantments that met my every whim, I wouldn't leave either, even if no one was keeping me there."

It was like she'd asked to see my hand, then sliced me across the palm.

"I'm only curious"—she went on—"what made you return now?"

The silence was worse than any I'd experienced at the castle.

"The forest was burning," I said at last. I'd almost forgotten about the smoke. "I thought you were in danger."

"How considerate." Astra smiled. "We thought you were in danger for six months—perhaps dead. But I'm glad you eased your own fears at the first sign." She pushed her chair back and stood. "Oh, and the forest hasn't burned, as far as I can tell. The evidence would be hard to hide. But maybe it was an enchanted fire."

An enchanted forest, actually. But the response would have been petty, even if it was true. Astra had always been good at turning the conversation so it was impossible to beat her last word. It was a trait Stephan shared.

If the worst part about the castle had been its silence, I'd underestimated the best—living without the constant barbs and attacks, the need to be so witty in order to stay on top. With Stephan at my side, I'd once dominated that game. I had no desire to play anymore.

So I did as Beast would. I remained silent.

And for once, the silence wasn't so bad. I had nothing to prove.

If you did walk in, Beast whispered in my memory, *it's no obligation to stay.*

That evening, Father asked me to read from his book of scripture. He could have read to the family himself, so I did not know if it was for my sake or his own that he asked me. Either way, I took the heavy leather volume and sat angled to the firelight in order to see the pages, and I read of the creation of the world, of light out of darkness, of the rolling back of the ocean that left the beach to breathe.

I thought Beast would have liked to hear the stories.

Rob and Astra excused themselves first, already yawning. Callista stayed longer, though after she nodded off once, she kissed Father's cheek and followed Astra to bed. I could have stopped reading then, but I continued, just Papa and me by the fire. He added a log as if he wanted things to keep going as well.

I noticed the gold rose on the mantel, kept in a small vase even though it needed no water. I paused to ask why he hadn't sold it.

"I thought I would have to," Father admitted. "But it felt like selling my daughter."

Yet, we had food stores in the winter and chickens in the yard.

"Astra," he said, surprising me. "She had her best necklace stashed away. She came home one afternoon with three laying hens and arms full of food. She told me to keep the rose."

Perhaps Astra had more of Mother in her than I'd ever given her credit for.

Then I wondered how the world would have changed had she sold the necklace before Father went hunting. I would never have left my family. But I would never have seen the castle.

"Papa." I leaned forward, cradling the book to my chest,

shielding the heat that raged inside me. "If sin leads to goodness, is it still sin?"

I couldn't regret meeting Beast.

But neither could I be grateful for every step that had led me to the castle.

"You've been reading that book all night." Father nodded to the scriptures. "You tell me."

My fingers turned the pages back gently, searching the words. The prophets in the desert had no answer for me, the men choosing wives and offering sacrifices to God. But there was a boy, a boy sold by his own brothers into slavery, a boy who grew to save a nation, who still wept over the betrayal even when he was full grown.

"I think . . ." I swallowed. "I think God makes light out of darkness. But the darkness still exists."

Father nodded. "And beauty from ash, though it's ash still. The bad is not good, but through grace, we can make something good of it in the end."

Beauty from ash.

I settled once more into the book, and I read until my throat was dry, and then we sat in the silence.

And I felt no need to fill it.

CHAPTER 16

A few days later, Astra sweetly asked if I would help bring in firewood. While I loaded my arms in the shed, she watched me with a knowing smile.

"It won't gather itself," I said, because I knew I had to speak first.

"Tell me honestly, Beauty, what does the monster look like?"

It wasn't the direction of conversation I'd expected. A log slipped from my gloved fingers. The gloves were Rob's and much too large on my hands.

"He looks . . ." I hesitated, thinking of Beast's round yellow eyes and his velvet suit. Despite myself, I smiled. There was no way to explain him to Astra. She would never understand. "He has fur."

Fur? Beast would have said. *Not technically wrong, but suppose she imagines me as a rabbit.*

"Also ears," I added, biting my lip to hold the laughter. I grabbed the dropped log and added it to the pile balancing in the crook of my left arm. "Eyes, nose, mouth. Arms and legs. You know—the expected features of a beast."

This time, I could almost hear him laughing with me.

Astra saw no humor, and her scowl was as fierce as a beast herself. "You mock me."

And suddenly it wasn't Beast I thought of. It was Stephan, both of us trading jibes over Astra's head or mimicking her stiff posture and exaggerated laugh within her view at a party.

I was wrong. Beast wouldn't laugh. He didn't mock others.

"I'm sorry, Astra." I sobered. "We're so different, sometimes it's hard . . . I don't understand you, and I know you don't understand me."

"Don't tell me what I do and don't understand, Beauty. Your books don't make you an expert on everything."

It was the way it had always been—a few sentences' conversation with Astra made me want to pull my hair out. But she was still my sister.

"Why do you want to know about Beast?"

"Never mind. I already know what I need."

She gathered firewood with such ferocity, her stack caught up to mine as if a gust of wind had blown it into her arms all at once.

"Astra, are you . . . happy here?" It was such a foolish question that my face burned at once. I'd tried to think of anything to connect us, but it would have been better to stay silent. Beast never would have been so careless with his words.

"Happy?" she spat. "No, I'm not happy here. Who could be?"

I opened my mouth, though I would probably only make things worse, but she plowed over top of me. "And don't pretend you care when you ask only to rub it in. You came here from your castle bringing diamond dresses but still wearing rags to show us all how humble you are. How, even when surrounded by wealth, clever Beauty only cares about people and ideas. Clever Beauty's better than the rest of us, young and carefree and loved by every man in society—and the beasts too!"

My face flooded with heat.

I couldn't manage a sound.

Astra stalked from the shed, but I stayed, shivering in cold and rage, but ashamed too, because of the kiss Astra had seen, because of everything Astra had ever seen me do, every stupid word she'd ever heard me speak. She was a fool. But I was a fool too, and nothing I did would ever make it right.

Then I thought of Andre and Bastien, and with a deep breath, I followed her into the house.

She had already removed her cloak, and she held her hands extended to the fire.

"I'm sorry," I said. "I have said and done a lot of things just to be unkind to you, and I'm sorry."

She stared at me with such hatred that I flinched.

Then she left the room.

I kept my cloak on, and I went out to meet Rob. He finished his rounds for the moneylender in a fraction of the time with Honey, which meant he came home earlier and had more energy to help in the evenings. I met him on the road, and he dismounted, leading Honey as he listened to my story.

At the end of it, he only shrugged. "Astra is stubborn, and she won't be reasoned with unless she wants to be. Not only that, but you can give a million apologies, and she'll still bring the grudge back like a knife."

"Still, I acted like a child, and I feel bad."

Rob slung his arm around my shoulders and squeezed. "You were a child, Beauty. And I think you've grown a lot in these last months alone. I hardly recognize you."

"Beast is a good influence."

His eyes widened. After a moment, he said, "I'm waiting for the rest of the joke."

"No jest this time. Just honesty. I learned that from him."

"The way you defend him . . ." He frowned. "If I didn't know better, I'd say . . ."

"What?"

"Nothing. I need to see to Honey."

He led her into the stall, and I lingered behind.

My eyes traveled to the forest, to the towering trees that hid a white castle deep in its heart.

The morning of the winter celebration dawned cold and clear. I helped Callista in the kitchen while she slaved over the best pies she could make. Astra sewed in the front room, a plain dress, too simple to belong to the carriage owner.

Seeing it, Callista said, "You should borrow my extra dress for this evening, Beauty."

"There's no need. I have no one to impress."

In truth, I had no desire to attend at all. With every day away from Beast, I missed him more. I would bear out this celebration, and in the morning, I would return to the castle.

That was my decision, made at last. I could almost see the gates already.

But I could not leave this time without saying goodbye, so I squared my shoulders and asked for another private conversation with Father.

He waited for me to speak, but I couldn't say it without the need to explain.

"I'd like to tell you everything," I said. "About the beast."

His eyebrows lifted meaningfully. "I'd very much like to hear it."

We sat on his bed, and I told him all my suspicions of the beast's enchantment—the evidences that he was a man, that he did not come from the castle but from humble roots as a fisherman.

"I think he found a fairy and wished to be a prince," I said. "He was given a castle and all the trappings, but in trade, he became a beast."

"A prince by all accounts, but unable to enjoy any of it," Father murmured. "I have always distrusted magic. I have heard of too many good men gone mad simply in the search for it. To find it may be even worse."

"There's something else." I hesitated. "He's asked me . . . to marry him."

Father's eyes went wide as eggs, and for some reason, I felt a ridiculous pang of irritation. Probably on behalf of Beast.

"He is forced to ask," I said. "I believe an acceptance is the key to breaking his curse."

"Beauty, you are under no obligation to marry anyone, no matter how it would help them."

Hearing it from someone outside myself lifted a weight from my shoulders.

"Stay home with us." He patted my hand as if the matter was decided. "I pity the beast—or man—but your home is here. You've no need to spend another minute away and no obligation to anyone except yourself for how you spend your life."

My lips twitched. "Not even to you and Mama?"

"Not even to us," he said seriously. "Beauty, listen to me. I want you to be happy. If I could, I would give you all the happiness in the world. But I would never control your choices. I have one life to govern, as do you, and if I can teach you to govern yours well, then I've been a father."

I didn't know what to say.

I'd always thought I had a duty to my parents—to reflect well on them, to use the advantages they gave me. Society said a good girl took her father's status and married above it, bringing a new son to the family and climbing a rung higher in society. It was why Astra had never been satisfied with the common city boys, with the sons of tradesmen and merchants. Father was a merchant, so she had to marry into peerage. It was her duty.

But now that I thought about it, Father had never told me anything of the sort. If he mentioned marriage, it was to say that he loved my mother. If he mentioned duty, he spoke of things we had already committed ourselves to, of lessons and pursuits. He believed in keeping his promises.

A sudden desire seized my chest, a need to understand.

"Why did you marry Mother?"

A faint smile crossed his face, creased the wrinkles at the corners of his eyes. "I met Rose when I was near twenty, and she was just turned sixteen. She was fiery and extravagant. The air around her was brighter than the rest of the world. And I loved her."

"Was she a lady?" I'd never thought to ask. I knew my mother hadn't spoken to her parents, but I'd never asked about that either.

"She was, and her father disapproved of her marrying an unproven merchant yet to make his fortune. She married me anyway."

There was nothing my mother loved more than the wealth to buy fine gowns and the opportunity to display such attire in society while giggling over feasts with other gossipy ladies.

Nothing she loved more, that is, except my father.

"Were you ever afraid"—I swallowed—"she'd be different after marriage?"

"Different how?"

"That she would change. That you'd see a side of her you'd never seen before. That you would regret marrying her."

"Well, she did change, Beauty. And so did I."

My heart shot into my throat.

He laughed and patted my shoulder. "People change, dear girl. It's in our nature. And of course I didn't know all there was to know about Rose before I married her. She had more impatience than I'd ever imagined and a sharp tongue that knew just how to wound. But she also had more generosity in her than I'd imagined. And when I saw her doting on you children, sacrificing her pride by making silly faces to earn baby giggles, I loved her more than ever before."

My chest was tight, trapping my breath. "But how did you know it would be worth it?"

"I didn't know. I only loved her enough to take the risk. It was like building my fortune: risks and rewards."

Not very comforting now, considering the bankruptcy.

"I loved Stephan at the start," I whispered. It was sour on my tongue to admit.

"I am sorry to hear that." He rested his hand on my head. "If I could protect you from risk, I would. If I could have every risk you took turn to your good, I would. I never wanted you to know half the horrors of the world you already know. You're too young."

I leaned into him with a sigh. "I am a thousand years old. I only look young on the outside."

"Don't say that. It would make me a thousand-plus years old, and I feel ancient as it is." He kissed the top of my head. "Now, come, it's a celebration tonight. No time for gloomy thoughts. You'll save me a dance, won't you?"

I nodded, trying not to think of Stephan bowing over my hand, leading me to the dance floor.

CHAPTER 17

That evening, we all trudged through the snow together until we reached the Merrells' barn. I was introduced to the family—"Good heavens, I didn't know you were hiding another daughter in that house!"—and I curtsied to Callista's fiancé, Thomas, who was a tall, broad-shouldered man, though not as tall as Beast.

"Beauty." He had a smile as broad as his shoulders. "Interesting name."

"I have also been known to answer to the call of Whimsy."

He frowned, and Callista hurriedly shooed me away before I could twist the mind of her love into knots.

A large table had been moved into the barn, and on it was piled all the food. It was to be feast first, dancing second. I sat next to Rob, watching him as we ate. There were several other young ladies present, and certainly they could not all be engaged. Yet Rob showed no interest in any.

"Have you spoken to Eva?" I asked, voice low.

His smile faded. Perhaps he wouldn't answer. In the past, I'd deflected serious matters with jest.

"Her father won't permit me near the house," he said at last.

His apprenticeship with a moneylender meant less pay than trade work would have brought, but more opportunity for social recognition in the future.

Risks and rewards, I heard my father say.

An apprenticeship took years. Eva might be married to someone else before he finished. Rob was already twenty-six, old enough to incur society's disapproval for not taking a wife. And suppose he did marry her, only to lose her as Father had lost Mother.

"You're very brave." I swallowed.

He frowned at me. "You're brave too, Beauty. If there's one thing all the Actons have in common, it's reckless bravery."

Hadn't I gambled too much of my life already in recklessness?

We finished the meal, and the music struck up a merry rhythm. Callista and Thomas were first on the barn floor, twirling and laughing like no one was watching. My sister had a glow to her cheeks I'd never seen before, and for a moment, a pain stabbed so deep I was certain something had pinned my organs to my spine.

Rob slung an arm around my shoulders. "I'm jealous too. It's what you do about it that matters."

"I think I'll ask my brother to dance."

"Excellent choice."

My brother wasn't very tall, and he wasn't broad-shouldered. In fact, there was nothing incredibly striking about him at all, at least to society's glance. But he was honest, and he was considerate. I wished he could have carried it as a pennant, an announcement to the world. I wished all people had a flag above their heads announcing them as charitable or unkind, thoughtful or bitter. Then we could all measure our standards by rulers with true weight.

Rob spun me around until I was laughing like Callista, and we stepped on each other's toes and didn't care. Country dances had no formality or rigidity, only the joy of music in the air and breath in the lungs. And soon enough, Rob and I had our arms lifted in an arch, the end of a line the others danced through, and above the laughter and the lute was Mr. Merrell's voice, pure and booming.

Lolly Lyla at the door
Wonder who she's looking for
Dance, my darling, all the day
Her poor boy has gone away.

I thought of a shining ballroom and a cheerful harpsichord. I wondered if Andre liked to dance.

When the music turned to a carol, Callista found us in the small crowd, dragging her fiancé, and then I had Rob on one side and Papa on the other, with Callista after that, and then Thomas, all of us holding hands as part of the growing circle, chanting back our answers to Mrs. Merrell who was leading the carol, all of us spinning around her like planets orbiting the sun.

Astra never joined the circle. She stood beside the door of the barn, and whenever my eyes caught hers, she gave an unnerving smile.

Just as I determined to ignore her, she drew my gaze again, and this time—

—Stephan stood with her.

I froze.

My father dragged at my arm, still caught up in the dance, and Rob plowed into me, but nothing could knock me off my feet. I had been rooted to the spot, and I felt the creeping vines all the way up to my neck, holding my head in place, holding my eyes on his.

I was the start of the commotion, but I wasn't the end of it. As the circle fractured, people noticed, and then came whispers of "the lord baron" until everyone stilled and the music died.

"Oh, please." Stephan's voice was loud in the closed area, his wave magnanimous. "Don't stop on my account. I'm only passing through."

Hesitantly, the festivities resumed, but my family did not rejoin them. The Merrells welcomed the future baron to their humble celebration, offered him what was left of the feast, their faces pale and embarrassed at the meagerness of it, then relieved at his refusal.

And all the while, his eyes were on me.

And my heart was in his grasp.

And he was squeezing tighter.

When he moved toward me, I gripped my ring. But before I could turn it, Rob stepped forward.

"That's far enough, my lord," he said, his expression pleasant even though his voice was as cold as the winter outside.

Stephan actually came to a halt, shock evident on his face. "I beg your pardon, peasant. Did you just give me an order?"

Rob did not budge, and now my father stood with him.

Off to the side, Callista wrung her hands, glancing at me, until she finally took my hand and pulled me back a step.

My jaw hung open as much as Stephan's did.

"Well, so much for the warm welcome," he drawled at last, glancing over his shoulder at Astra. Her cheeks flamed.

"You have my answer concerning my daughter," Father said firmly. "It hasn't changed."

Astra joined Stephan's side. "Father, be reasonable. Beauty's marriage to Stephan will make all our fortunes again. Callista and I will have dowries. Rob will have status."

"You've been speaking behind my back." Father stood straight, his face stormy. "And he's promised all this, has he?"

"Of course," Stephan purred. "Anything for family."

I was a carving at a carnival, and Stephan was the merchant in the stall, bartering my worth. Two dowries and the social standing to match—what a bargain. How selfish of me for never considering how my misery could buy my family's happiness.

But even if they hated me for it, I couldn't.

And I couldn't stay silent. It was not in me to die with fear in my throat.

I opened my mouth, but Father spoke first.

"The answer remains."

Rob nodded.

Callista's hand tightened on mine.

And my eyes stung.

Stephan's smile thinned. He looked past Rob's shoulder and said to me, "Come now, my Beauty. You can't be this selfish."

But I could.

Because the people I loved supported me.

"I'll never marry you, Stephan," I said, with more force and power than I had at his last proposal.

I wished saying it would break some kind of spell, would fill me with confidence and banish his ghost. It didn't. My hands still trembled. But I felt something, some kind of settling, like the tide washing out and leaving the beach to breathe. And that was enough.

"Sounds clear to me," said Rob.

"I own you," Stephan said to Father, a dare in his gleaming eyes.

But Father only shook his head. "The baron may own these lands, my taxes, and my allegiance, but not my daughter. If there is a problem, I'll find another land. I have no fortune to lose."

Stephan narrowed his eyes on me, but I would not help him talk his way around Father this time.

"There is a piece of me," I said, "taken by force. That is yours. Content yourself with it. My hope is that it will become a fire, and on your lowest night, it will turn on you and scorch your conscience."

But if not, I would still live my life looking forward.

Beauty from ash.

"Live your life in the dirt," Stephan snarled. "Even if you come on your knees begging, I'll never take you back."

He turned away, and in a rush, Astra caught his arm.

"Marry me, my lord," she pleaded.

He shook her off with force, never glancing back.

A hush fell over the party, all eyes focused on us. Father smoothed things over the best anyone could, and then we took our leave, allowing everyone else to gossip without concern. Even Callista seemed eager to go, probably to escape the flood of questions her fiancé would have.

We were all silent on the walk home, faces turned against the wind, steps crunching loudly in the snow.

But even in the cold, I felt warm.

Upon arriving home, Father pulled Astra into private conversation, his expression as bleak as the storm outside. For once, I pitied my eldest sister.

As Callista and I readied for bed, she grabbed my hand once more. She didn't speak. Then I hugged her, and we just held each other.

I'd planned to leave in the morning, but in that moment, I couldn't. A few more days couldn't hurt. Another week, perhaps. However long this feeling could stay alive.

But the next morning changed it all.

CHAPTER 18

I helped Callista with breakfast, both of us smiling and joking as we hadn't done in years. Rob was helping Father, so I cooked the bread myself, watching carefully that it didn't burn.

"Perhaps tomorrow we can buy a real loaf from the baker," Callista suggested. "To celebrate."

I didn't know what exactly we were celebrating, but I liked the idea. She stirred the porridge, and I finished the bread and delivered it to the table. Then I reached for my ring.

Only it wasn't there.

Everything warm in the world chilled.

"Beauty, what's wrong?"

I overturned every object on the counter. Had I somehow knocked it to the floor and not noticed? I dropped to my hands and knees.

"Beauty!" Callista craned her neck to look at me as I scampered around the floor.

"My ring! Where is it?"

She looked away, but the flush betrayed her.

"Callista, where is it?"

"I saw Astra take it." She sighed. "With everything that happened yesterday . . . I didn't want to see you two fight again. And anyway, you don't care for jewelry and fancy things. Let Astra have it."

My heart twisted.

"Astra!" I shouted, dragging myself to my feet. "Astra, don't!"

I ran toward the bedroom, but it would be too late. Three turns was easy. Three turns and she'd vanish in a blink with no one watching.

Loved by every man in society, she'd accused me. And the beasts too. She'd tried to claim Stephan and couldn't. Now it was only the beasts left.

Once more, I remembered kissing Stephan to anger Astra.

I remembered how Beast could not help but ask his question.

How the castle drew people in.

I searched the small cottage from top to bottom, overturning two chairs in my haste. Astra was not there. Outside, a light snow had fallen, and no footprints marred it but those belonging to Father and Rob.

I ran to the edge of the forest and stood there, panting, breath fogging and fading. The dark trees looked down on me, and every shadow seemed to laugh.

Somewhere in those dark trees, there was a bright castle.

A glimmer of blue flickered before me, and then the fairy and I stood eye to eye. She smiled, but it didn't reach those inhuman blue orbs.

"Have you a wish now?" she asked.

I had been cornered. I thought of sitting on Honey,

watching the storm above the trees, hearing Beast say they came alive to keep even him out. Had anyone tried to force their way through at all? Had it all been a fairy's trap for me?

"I can grant you safe passage," the fairy offered. "Only say the word."

"My father passed through once," I choked out.

"The castle has no need of an occupant," she said, "if it already has one."

I saw the truth in her empty eyes.

I was not Orla Byrne, pirate queen. I was not undefeated in combat, nor did I possess any skill in it, and skill would not defeat enchantments anyway. As soon as I entered the forest, the trees would hook me with root and limb and drag me screaming into the wet earth. I would never make it.

But I could not let Astra marry Andre.

She would do it to spite me. Not for the riches and the castle—for spite.

And he would be kind to her because my beast was kind down to his soul, and that would never change.

"Have you a wish?"

"I do." I swallowed. "But not for you."

I ran back to the house. I traded my boots for Callista's, lined with rabbit fur and warmer than mine. I had borrowed her cloak the day before, and I wrapped it around me again, pulling the wool hood snugly around my face.

"Beauty, what are you doing?" Callista's voice was hysterical.

"I have to get back to him."

"Astra freed you! Can't you see that? She's been miserable

here. Let her at least have a castle if she'll abide the beast who owns it."

"He's mine," I snarled, selfish and possessive and uncaring.

You are selfish, he said. *And so am I.*

Before I'd left the castle, he'd asked me to marry him even though he'd already asked that day. That wasn't the enchantment. That was him. I'd known, and I'd listened to fear.

But I wasn't afraid anymore.

A feeling nudged me, and I checked the gold-trimmed chest that was still in the front room. After I'd pulled Father's book from it, it had been empty, but now it held two sword hilts. I drew out the weapons one at a time like drawing swords from stone. Though I'd never seen the shining silver blades before, I knew at once they had previously been wooden. They belonged to two pirates who belonged together, and they were the finest fairy silver, forged in a dragon's breath.

I borrowed one of Rob's belts and strapped the spare sword to my waist, gripping the one I knew to be Ruiner.

Callista had run for Father, and he burst into the house, panting, just as I made to leave. Rob was with him; he wouldn't leave for his route until after breakfast.

"Beauty, what . . . what is this?" Father demanded.

Meeting his eyes evenly, I said, "Astra has taken my ring to the castle. I will go through the woods."

"Foolish girl," he murmured. I did not know which of us he spoke of. Perhaps both.

I could see in his face that he would wrap me in a hug, coax me back to the fire, persuade me to stay.

So I said the truth, "Father, I love him."

For all the thorns I'd faced, at last I'd found the roses.

Callista's eyes doubled in size. She pressed her hands to her mouth in such shock, I might have announced my new life's calling as a pirate queen. Rob's jaw swung open like it had been unhinged. Father only shook his head.

"My whimsical Beauty." His forehead creased with worry. "You have never been content with a simple world."

"I can be no one but myself, Papa." I smiled.

"You can't go." Callista grabbed Father's arm. "She can't go! She's only just come back."

"And she'll come back again." Father reached for me. "Promise me, girl."

I hugged him. "I promise."

"I'm going with you," Rob said.

"No, Rob." He would be fired if he did not show up to work with no explanation. The family couldn't afford that. We argued, but in the end, he saw reason.

"Take Honey," he said.

And I couldn't argue that.

Rob saddled her, whispered something in her ear, which Honey answered with a sharp nod, her mane flopping against her neck.

Then I climbed up, and Father handed me my sword, looking all the while like he was biting his tongue to keep from ordering me back to the house.

"I'll be fine," I said, as much for my sake as for theirs.

I faced the dark wood, sword in hand, staring down the towering trees from Honey's saddle. She shied, stamping anxiously.

"I know, girl," I murmured. "But I have to."

I took a deep breath and dug in my heels. Into the woods we went.

The forest swallowed me immediately, closing around me like a curtain, and when I glanced back, I could no longer see the cottage, though it couldn't have been more than fifty feet away. I patted Honey's neck, gripped my sword more tightly, and pressed on. If there was something I could do to reason or bargain with the enchantments in the trees, I could not think of it, so I remained silent.

The branches at first arched above my head, and the path between the trees—though not packed down by travel—was at least clear of jutting roots. But as we progressed, the branches grew more oppressive, lowering and thickening until I had to hunker toward Honey's neck to avoid the thin wooden fingers. Creeping roots began to appear as bumps on the frosted path, waiting to catch Honey's hooves. Though I felt the urgency of my situation, we had to pick our way forward with caution.

Then I heard the howl.

Honey's ears pricked, and her eyes rolled. She strained against the reins as another howl echoed the first. My palms began to sweat within my gloves. I threw back my hood, squinting in the shadows between trees, but nothing moved.

I knew nothing of predators except what I'd read, and the knowledge jumbled in my mind. But it didn't matter since my cursory study of wolves could not hold up against whatever beasts might roam an enchanted forest.

I searched the forest, looking for a glimmer of gold for the gates or a flash of color for the gardens, anything that would signal the castle. But it was only black tree after black tree.

Honey strained again. I forced her to keep the slow, methodical pace. If she tripped and broke a leg, we would both be done for.

The chill increased with the depth of the forest. My breath clouded the air, and when I pressed my nose to the bare skin of my wrist between glove and sleeve, it felt like a rounded icicle.

Another howl.

Closer this time, I was certain.

Honey danced sideways, and I tucked her head firmly, murmuring in what I hoped was a comforting tone. Unfortunately, she'd brought me right to the trunk of a tree, and as I tried to soothe her, one of its branches snaked around my chest, almost pulling me from the saddle.

I shrieked, grabbing for Honey's mane.

Responding to my loud voice and my fear, Honey reared, loosening the branch's hold. With my other hand, I swung Ruiner and managed to slice the grasping branch.

There was another shriek—not from me. A sound more creaking wood than voice.

I wheeled Honey away from the tree and watched in wide-eyed amazement as the branch I'd sliced caught fire. It was a slow, meaty burn, like the little ball of flame was a fire demon intent on chewing every bit of bark, savoring the fuel it consumed. The branch whipped back and forth, the wood of the tree groaning and shrieking, and all the while, that fist of flame crept and grew and reached out to grasp other branches.

And then the whole forest woke.

Suddenly, every tree was reaching. The ground rolled with roots rising like ocean waves. Trunks curved and bent as branches grasped for me, for Honey. Honey bellowed in fear, and I gave her free rein. There was no choice and no option for a creeping, careful pace now.

She bolted, winding through the trees like wind itself. I clung to her neck, as low as I could manage. Thin fingers snagged in my cloak, my hair. I slashed with Ruiner when they did, and each time a new fire started, the trees around it reared away.

At any moment, I expected Honey to stumble, expected to be sent crashing to the ground, but she somehow kept her footing on the rolling waves. I remembered that she was enchanted too—a part of the beast's castle as much as the rose gardens.

"Honey, take me home!" I shouted. "Take me to the castle!"

I held tight, fingers knotted in her mane, trusting her to find her way through the trees. She carried me, and I cleared our path with fire.

And a small part of me—just a corner—felt like a triumphant pirate queen.

Then a snarling shadow leapt at me and caught my cloak. I choked as the bone fastener dragged against my throat until the thin cord holding it snapped. I had to grab with both hands to keep my seat, and my sword fell away into the roiling tree roots.

More snarls echoed around us, somehow keeping pace even as Honey flew.

I felt the second sword bouncing against my leg as we galloped. If I spared a hand to reach for it, I could be knocked from the saddle. But if I did not, the next wolf might leap at Honey rather than me—her legs or her neck.

I untangled my right hand from Honey's mane and twisted to reach for the sword. As I turned, I saw gleaming red eyes and a sleek silver coat, closer to me than the closest pitching tree.

Just as the wolf leapt, I dragged the sword from the knot that served as a sheath.

And I swung.

The shock of impact almost knocked the weapon from my hand, and my left foot slipped from its stirrup. But the wolf's fur caught fire just as the trees had. The wolf crashed to the ground with a yelp, and we galloped away.

Then I saw a glimmer of white through the trees ahead, too solid to be snow.

I clung to Honey's mane with my free hand, dug my left knee into her side when I could not regain the stirrup, and swung the sword at every reaching branch, every snarling shadow. I lit the forest ablaze and kept the wolves at bay and fought with everything I had to buy us that last minute we needed.

Then as abruptly as leaping from a cliff, we burst from the forest.

The trees retreated. The golden gates swung open.

And all at once, it was spring.

CHAPTER 19

I dropped the second sword in relief as Honey cantered to a stop, both of us heaving for breath. When I swung down from the saddle, my knees gave out, bringing me hard to the ground. Honey nosed my hair, then snorted in my face. I dragged myself up and staggered toward the castle.

The doors opened before I even raised a hand, as if letting me know I hadn't been forgotten. My heart lifted.

"Beast!" I tried to shout, but my voice only rasped.

Inside, I grabbed the banister and hauled myself up to the second floor, tripping twice over the stairs.

But when I reached my room, I felt the winter chill of the outside world all over again.

Where the door had once said "Beauty," framed by carved roses, it now said "Astra," framed by faceted gems. The door was no longer wood at all. It was solid gold, and it would not open at my touch.

The castle may have recognized me, but I was no longer its resident.

I wheeled from the door and ran to the library, but it was deserted. Astra would never be in the library, but I'd hoped

Beast might be. I forced myself to stop long enough to think, and I realized Astra would be in the grandest room she could find. She would want vaulted ceilings and chandeliers and everything that spoke of a palace.

I hurried back down the stairs to the main ballroom.

I burst through the doors and saw them immediately: Beast hunkered near the harpsichord and Astra standing in full confidence a few feet away. She smiled to see me. His eyes widened.

Astra was in the silver dress, glowing like a princess in the sunlight from the tall glass windows. I was like a forest demon crawling from my bush lair, my dress tattered from the reaching branches, my face scratched and bleeding.

"Beauty, you're just in time," Astra said. "This beast has asked me to marry him, and I'm so pleased you've come to hear my answer."

Beast looked at me with agonized yellow eyes. "Beauty, I didn't—"

"Astra, please," I panted.

But she'd already said it, head raised high, chin tilted up: "Yes, ugly beast, I will marry you."

"No!" I shouted, as if force alone could negate it, could hold the enchantment at bay. Even though it was too late, I ran for him, and Beast met me in the middle, catching me gently as I sagged. His claws pressed into my arms like thorns, but I only clung tighter.

Astra laughed. "It's too late, Beauty. How does it feel when someone takes something from you?"

"Please, don't. Don't marry her." It didn't make sense to beg him as if he had any choice in the matter, yet it was all I could think to do.

He was babbling just the same. "She told me you sent her. She told me this was what you wanted."

"My sister's very familiar with secrets and lies," Astra said.

It was lucky for her I'd lost both swords.

I waited for a transformation, for Beast to vanish, for any kind of change at all, but the seconds passed, and nothing happened.

"What is this?" Astra demanded at last. "I've broken the curse. Beauty, I heard you with Father. You insisted there was a curse."

I couldn't explain it, but I was glad all the same. Gently, Beast released my left arm, pressed his first knuckle to my cheek, where it came away streaked with blood.

"You came through the forest?" he whispered.

"I am an undefeated pirate queen. I did what I had to."

I was afraid. I'd thought I wasn't, but when I looked at him and thought of marriage and love and everything that lay along the road of life, the fear was still there, like orange embers in my belly, waiting to be stoked. But the waiting fire was weaker than the overwhelming current that had pulled me back to his side.

"Ask me again." I curled my hand around his, held tight. "I'll say yes this time."

He shook his head. "You don't have to."

"I want to."

"No!" Astra shrieked. "He's mine. He asked me, and I said yes. This time, I've won."

"I'm still afraid of the unknown," I said, my eyes never leaving his, "and afraid of the past too. But you're worth the risk. And I don't care what changes—the castle, the gardens, the library. It can all go. I don't care. You're the kindest man I've ever met, and I'll take the risk to be with you forever."

"Beauty . . ."

I saw the fear in him too.

"Ask me. If you want. If you love me."

"I do," he whispered.

And here I'd thought my heart could rise no higher.

"You don't understand," he pressed. "I am as bad as the man who stole your confidence and freedom. I also tried to seize what wasn't mine. I brought my punishment upon myself."

"You reached for a rose." But I smiled as I said it. "We all have some greed in us, and yours is nothing like his."

The fact that he hesitated said it all—that he thought of me when I offered to give him freedom, that my feelings meant more than his escape.

A strange prince indeed. One worth loving.

"Stop this!" Astra grabbed at his arm, but she could not move him.

"Beauty, will you marry me?"

"Yes"—I laughed, because everything was different this time, because everything was right—"with all my heart."

"Nothing will happen," Astra sneered. "For all your talk, your beast is just a beast."

But even as she said it, a tingling spread beneath my fingers, sharpening almost to needles. I let out a small gasp, releasing Beast even though I didn't want to.

A faint blue glow swept across Beast's dark fur, leaving pale skin in its wake. His claws and pointed ears and fangs disappeared, leaving human hands, human ears, and a gentle human smile. His yellow eyes softened to a beautiful hazel, nearly amber.

The change was so instant that when I blinked and shook my head, I could have been convinced he'd looked this way all along. A human in a baggy velvet suit.

He hadn't shrunk much—he was still a foot taller than I was—and I took comfort in that.

Not everything had to change.

He turned his palms upward, staring at them. Then he pressed his hands to his face.

I smiled.

He reached for me, pulled me close. I raised on my toes to kiss him. He was as gentle in the kiss as he was in everything else. This was no consuming fire. It was comfort. Safety. And a little thrill all the way down to my soul.

My sister's shriek in the background reminded me she was there.

As Beast and I broke apart, another blue glow caught my eye.

"Here is completion," said the fairy, deadpan. "Never again may you claim a wish."

Beast angled himself between me and the fairy, a sweet gesture.

"I've learned my lesson," he said.

"I suppose some do." She cocked her head at me. "A wish is still available to you. The world and its riches are open."

I threaded my fingers through his. "I have all I need."

"Give me a wish, fairy!" Astra burst out, flaming red from her cheeks to her ears. "Make me more beautiful than she."

"Astra, don't!" I grabbed my sister's arm, but she shook me off.

A spark of life entered the fairy's eyes. When she smiled, she showed small, pointed fangs. "Any wish is available. Only name it."

"I wish to be so beautiful, wealthy men propose at the sight of me."

"You don't know what you're doing," Beast said. But our protests fell on deaf ears.

"Wish granted."

The fairy twirled, her gossamer dress shedding flakes of blue that coated Astra head to foot in a glow.

My sister had always been beautiful. When I was little, I would ask to brush and braid her hair, admiring all the while how the shining auburn caught the sun just like Mother's did, while mine was an earthy brown unable to hold the light. Her true smile was rare, but it was radiant, full of mischief and mystery, scrunching her eyes and nose.

But at the fairy's spell, she became almost inhuman. Her skin was more like porcelain than flesh, smooth and shaped like a doll's. Her hair took on volume and shine, but it was no longer from catching the sun. Now it glowed from within. Her once-auburn curls now turned a slightly different shade at every moment, mesmerizing and unnerving. Her cheeks held a perfect light blush, her lips a perfect red hue, her eyes an unavoidable gaze.

It was terrifying to see in her everything that was Astra and yet nothing of my sister at all.

Astra looked at Beast expectantly, but he held me closer to him.

"It didn't work," she said to the fairy. She must have tried for a scowl, but even her petulance was beautiful, her perfect lower lip pushed in the slightest pout and not a wrinkle on her forehead. "You lied to me."

"He," the fairy said pointedly, "is not wealthy."

Astra stared around at the grand ballroom with its gold ceilings.

"Three years ago"—Beast spoke to me, not her, and there was color in the tips of his human ears—"I hunted down a fairy and wished to be prince of my own kingdom. She gave me everything a prince would have: a castle and grounds, fashion, wealth. But I became a monster, unable to go out in society, surrounded by an impenetrable forest. And although the castle kept itself as if run by a hundred servants, I was alone, a prince with no one to see or know, with a kingdom that quite literally belonged to only me."

The fairy nodded, apparently pleased with herself.

"I regretted my wish almost instantly." His voice had lowered, and he looked at our clasped hands rather than my eyes. "But when I asked to go back, I was told . . ."

"Fairies can't rescind wishes. Only completion can," I said.

He nodded.

I narrowed my eyes on the fairy. "So you forced him to propose to everyone?"

She only puffed up her chest. "Every wish has a completion. To the one who wished for solitary luxuries, he must accept sharing poverties."

"You could have shared with Astra." I remembered telling him how he would do better to marry her. She'd said yes.

He gave a small smile as he tucked my filthy, windswept hair away from my face. "I didn't truly want to."

If you need me to be a beast, he'd once told me, *then I'll be a beast.*

How long had he loved me while I was still battling ghosts?

I looked up. "But the castle is still here."

"It will be until you step outside," the fairy said. "And the gardens and gates will be there until you step outside them. The forest will remain, but it will be ordinary, as it was before."

"Well, Beauty." Astra tried for what I imagined was a cruel smile, but her new face could only make a dazzling one. "You lost after all. He's nothing but an ordinary man, poor as an empty flour sack."

Beast lowered his eyes again, and I squeezed his hand.

"Nevertheless," I said, "I think he'll make a good cabin boy."

He kissed my fingers, spreading warmth through every bit of me.

"What's your name?" I asked. "Your real name."

"Andre Wolf."

I'd thought it might be, and yet it was still jarring to hear.

"Sneaky wee beastie." No wonder he'd stared at me with such tenderness whenever I called him Andre. "I'm afraid I'm not truly Orla."

"I like Beauty just fine."

And I believed him.

The fairy fluttered around Astra, blue glitter falling with

her every move. "Should you ever desire to find completion, you must be drawn to ugliness. But I do hope you'll be satisfied with your wish. It makes the watching so much more enjoyable. Come! I will take you to a place full of wealthy men."

The fairy disappeared, and so did Astra.

I reached for her but grasped only empty air.

My eyes stung. With all our history, with everything she'd attempted that morning alone, it was surely stupid of me to cry for my selfish sister.

But Andre held me, and he said nothing of the sort.

"I'm sorry," he said, as if it were somehow his fault. "She'll regret her wish soon enough. She'll come home."

It was kind of him. I wasn't sure he was right, but either way, I couldn't be responsible for Astra's actions and choices. My own were hard enough to bear.

I took a steadying breath and wiped my eyes. When I looked up, Andre was staring at me. "What is it?"

"I'm only . . ." He shook his head. "I'm only the son of a fisherman."

I smiled. "And I'm only the daughter of a bankrupt merchant. There are still books in the world and plenty of whimsy. I imagine we'll get along just fine."

He kissed me again, even more tender this time and lingering. I waited for myself to regret my decision, but I only became more certain it was right.

When we finally broke for air, I said, "It's winter in the world."

"Is it?" His eyes lit up. "I've longed to see the snow."

I took his hand, and we left the castle together. When we

looked back, it was gone, not even foundations remaining to show where it had once stood, only another garden of blooming flowers. I would miss the library and my armchair, the stubborn wardrobe and my sleek violin. But I had the memories.

And above all else, I had Andre.

Honey waited at the gate, and I hoped that meant the gifts remained—that Father still had his scriptures, Callista her candle. The castle's enchantments were not so stingy as to retract the magic that had passed its gates. Perhaps somewhere out there in the woods, there was even a shining sword of fairy steel. Perhaps the next time a girl went running out at night, crying and hoping to be eaten, she would instead find a sword to lift.

Andre helped me into the saddle and then climbed up behind me, his arms around me warm and secure.

"Well, Orla," he whispered in my ear, "where shall we sail to?"

I shivered and leaned into him. "There's a small cottage beyond the forest, belonging to the Acton family. It's said to contain the map to the fountain of youth, and as you know, this year marks my quest for it."

"Then to the cottage it is."

The golden gate opened before us, and as we galloped out, the fence and the gardens melted into pristine, unbroken snow.

It was a whimsical idea to think they'd been there at all.

EPILOGUE

It's not true what the folktale says. We did not live happily ever after.

Not for the reason you think—not because we lived *unhappily.* Only because "happily ever after" is a neat bow to tie up a tale, an ending to a thing which requires one.

In truth, we were only beginning. Each new day, each new hour, each new smile—and Andre's smile still had a bit of whimsy in it, a bit of crooked lift on one side more than the other—we were beginning again and discovering a wide new world.

Everything began with that trip home, when Honey broke through the trees and my anxious family swarmed us. Introductions were made, and though Andre towered over my father and brother both, he bowed with such timid hope that he seemed like a child in Father's shadow. He needn't have worried. Father said nothing of the gold rose or the first visit to the castle, only welcomed him as his own. When he thanked him for his care of me, Andre and I both turned red.

As it was my duty to fill the silence, I announced our engagement, which Father accepted in stride, Rob tried and almost managed to smile at, and Callista seemed to take like a chicken swallowing an apple core.

Eventually came the question: "Where's Astra?"

And then it was a heavy household for all.

At last, Rob told Andre, "I have clothes you can borrow."

They didn't fit, of course, being several inches short at wrists and ankles. It was like Andre had grown up overnight without informing his clothing, but it was better than the baggy velvet suit.

Father appraised the velvet with merchant eyes, admiring the rich color most of all, until he announced he knew who would purchase it. While he was in town, Rob arranged for Andre to stay with the Merrells, though Callista blanched at the idea of my beast and her fiancé sharing a roof.

"What if he maintained the appetite?" she asked.

I restrained any biting comments; losing one sister in a day was already one too many.

In the end, the arrangement worked well. According to Andre, Thomas was cheerfully welcoming—"Broad smile?" I asked. "Huge," he said, eyes wide—and promised to arrange for Andre to take a position at the shipyard with him. It was good work for a man already acquainted with ships. Sometimes Andre would joke with me that he was crafting a replacement for his tragically sunk *Sea Witch*.

"Would you prefer fishing?" I asked on one walk home.

Where we had once taken afternoons together, now it was evenings. I met him every day after work, and we walked the snowy path to the forest, hand in hand, breath clouding the air.

"I'm content to remain on land," Andre said, "until my pirate queen next sets sail."

I did have a secret voyage planned to find his mother, but it was not yet time.

After all, there was another beginning around the corner.

Everything began with our wedding. The world had melted enough for land to be tilled, and though the mornings still dawned clear and crisp, I welcomed the bite as it reminded me of white castles.

Father kissed my forehead and told me that even now, the morning of my wedding, I could change my mind. Strangely enough, that was all I needed to move forward.

He told Callista the same—because it was her wedding day as well.

When Father had first suggested we share a wedding day, I'd told Callista she could say no. It was a practical suggestion because even a modest celebration took funds to host, but I had never been one to bow to practicality. Andre and I would be happy enough to be married without a celebration at all.

When I told her as much, she snorted and said, "I'm your sister. Don't lie to me."

Though I wasn't sure exactly what lie I'd told, the plans moved forward: two weddings, one day.

Callista oversaw everything, preventing me from what she termed "self-sabotage," such as my attempt to have a plain, un-embroidered wedding dress. Though she couldn't talk me into anything so intricate as the beautiful songbirds trailing her own wedding skirt, she did convince me to add a thin pattern of roses along every hem. I finally agreed only because I thought my mother should be with me in some form on the most terrifyingly exciting day of my life.

Now I stood in that dress, and I gripped my sister's hands, and we looked at each other with the same kind of wide-eyed wonder, both of us silently asking if maybe it wouldn't be better to run after all because so much would change in this one day.

Or maybe it was just me.

"I thought you were in love once," she said, surprising me. "And I was wrong. But this time is different, isn't it?"

I nodded. "It is."

Where there had once been a fire inside me, now there was a quiet certainty, built by afternoons in a library and evenings on a frosty path.

The Merrells did not begrudge the addition of a second wedding to their barn. The guest list was the same, after all, with all the same mouths to feed and the same priest required to officiate.

We all stood outside for the ceremony, beneath an arch of willow branches that represented a willingness to bend when the storms of life inevitably raged against our new unions.

Andre's hair was a rich hickory in the sunlight, like the fur of a beast that was now only memory, and I saw in his eyes the same certainty I felt inside my heart.

The priest blessed our marriages and declared them valid in the eyes of God.

Callista burst into laughter as Thomas swept her off her

feet, spinning them both in dizzy circles while our family and friends cheered.

Andre only slid a wooden band onto my finger and gently pressed his lips to mine. While I was still breathless, staring at the ring, he traced his finger around it and then down my palm, sending shivers all the way to my core.

"The circle of eternity," he said quietly. "The existence that never ends."

It was a philosophical teaching. I must have shared it one afternoon, and he'd tucked the details away as he always did.

Suddenly, though I possessed all the words in the world, none were enough to describe everything he meant to me.

The wedding party lasted all afternoon, with feasting and wine, and enough dancing to regret all the feasting and wine. Callista sang in a way to shake the rafters and open a path to the heavenly chorus that surely harmonized. Her new husband was moved to tears, and his older brother tried to tease him for the display only to have his own cracked voice betray him.

Rob shook Andre's hand and gripped his shoulder, saying something I couldn't hear but that my husband later assured me was *mostly* not a threat.

My husband. As a fairy had once told me, I knew the weight in a word, and the more I ran "husband" through my mind while watching Andre's amber eyes and crooked smile, while feeling his hand in mine and his arm around me, the more I liked the weight of it.

Thomas had managed to secure a small house already, so as soon as the festivities ended, he and Callista set off. Andre and I were, quite literally, starting from the ground. With help, he'd laid the foundations as soon as the ground thawed, but it would be a while yet before we had walls and a roof. In the meantime, he and I had the room I'd previously shared with my sisters in the cottage.

Only once we were alone in it did I fully realize the weight in the word "husband."

Everything began with our wedding night, when I was trembling too heavily to even unbutton my dress, and Andre gathered me into his arms and whispered there was no rush. He traced the ring once more and told me there was time enough in eternity to wait until I was ready.

I didn't mean to, but I cried into his nightshirt because every time I thought I'd found the end to Stephan's path, it seemed to begin again, always in the worst places. But there was comfort in Andre's understanding—in his steady patience—and reason enough to keep walking.

Father accepted my husband like he'd had a second son all his life. He was particularly eager to address religious topics, and he found a more captive audience in Andre than Rob, because Andre could be prodded to read scripture for more than ten minutes at a time and never complained about being dragged to church, which Father did often after discovering his poor son-in-law's childhood had been robbed of any religious exposure.

Sometimes, Andre and I would lie awake in the dark of night, and he would recount whatever mountain of information my father had most recently buried him in, and we would sort through it together, forming our own questions and drawing our own conclusions.

As the nights passed, it grew easier to lay by his side with trust, until I even looked forward to waking in his arms.

"You *are* a prince," I told him once, squeezing his hand in the dark. My own barely trembled. "Your wealth is kindness and your castle, consideration."

"Hmm?" he murmured, half-asleep.

He snuggled closer, head knocking softly against mine.

I bit my lip, grinning to myself. "Nothing, wee beastie."

Though never hostile, Rob was more stubborn in his acceptance, as if waiting for some kind of sign to tell him his new brother-in-law was more than a barely trustworthy, reformed beast. The lightning must have struck without him even realizing because somewhere between helping Andre lay the foundation of our new home and helping him nail the shingles, my brother's smiles grew easy once more, even in Andre's company.

"Did you say something to him?" I asked curiously.

Andre only shrugged, reminding me that silence was still his companion more often than speech. A mystery, then, but I contented myself with the result. Even I couldn't expect to know every reason in life.

At last, the door was affixed and our home completed.

"One rickety hut," Rob said, dropping his hand on my shoulder. "You wanted it rickety, right?"

"It wouldn't be home otherwise," I agreed, though our new cottage was steady on its foundations.

And maybe I was too, because after Andre and I moved in, I kissed him that night and said I was ready.

Everything began with an adventure, and there were adventures aplenty—the adventures of a daily life, of working and saving, of gathering scattered notes of hope until we had a melody. Marriage was not always easy. We were both haunted by ghosts, though they took different forms.

At times, I caught Andre frowning down at his blistered hands or helped him dig slivers from his skin, and I reminded him it was only normal to miss a white castle and its comforts, no matter what price the comforts had cost.

At times, he caught me waking from a nightmare, and he rubbed my back until I could breathe again.

It was not always smooth sailing, but we faced the winds and we tackled the waves, a pirate queen and her strange prince.

That's the truth of how our story began: with storms and with sunlight.

And one more familiar element—

After we'd settled into our new home, Father stopped by one day with news from Callista. Apparently, she demanded a visit from her negligent sister. Father and I laughed, and I promised I'd make time to see her the next day, without fail. He returned to his fields, but he left something behind on the mantel, its gold petals shining.

A rose.

ACKNOWLEDGMENTS

This book would not have been possible without my support network of wonderful people. To mention just a few—

My beta readers: Rachel Bird, thank you for your endless enthusiasm and praise, and for making me really feel like I can write. Brooke Adams, thank you for reading a romance book, for giving me courage that if I can win you over to a "Beauty and the Beast" retelling, I can win anyone over. Constance Dalrymple, thank you for convincing me in chapter one that I had something unique to say. Ashlie Olson, thank you for loving this one so hard and sustaining me through every discouragement.

My family: Mom, thank you for encouraging my writing from day one and for paying my way through those first writing conferences. Brady, thank you for loving what I love, and when you don't, for loving me anyway. Thank you for being my own strange prince. There aren't words.

My mentors: Josh Allen, thank you for teaching me how to craft characters, how to take lessons from superheroes, how to own it all fearlessly. Above all, thank you for making me write over and over and over again. Lisa Mangum, thank you for your patience through the years, for encouraging me even when I gave you pages filled with cliches, for the rejections that sent me back to learn more and do it better. Thank you for being my friend and teaching me as much about life as you have about writing—I will always want to be you when I grow up.

My publishing team: A massive thank you to everyone who has helped this story go from a lonely document on my computer to a real book for real people to read. Lisa, again, for keeping all my words in line. Chris Schoebinger and Heidi Gordon, for championing my story through all the steps of production. (Chris, I believe you used the phrase "award-winning" at one point, so thank you for giving me a hundred years of fuel for happiness.) Richard Erickson, thank you for my enchanting cover, for bringing Beauty to life. Thanks to Breanna Anderl, for her typesetting work; and to Troy, Callie, and Hayley, for helping my book be seen.

Lastly but most importantly, thanks be to God. Not to conceitedly imply any divine hand on this work, but to acknowledge my gratitude for the belief that talents are divine, should be developed, and can make a difference. And my eternal gratitude for all the beliefs beyond that. Without them, without Him, I wouldn't be who I am.

DISCUSSION QUESTIONS

1. Fairy tales are told and retold. What do you think makes the story of Beauty and the Beast last? How does *Beauty Reborn* differ from other versions you've read or seen?
2. In the beginning, Stephan seems charming and romantic. Knowing what happens, what red flags stand out to you about his behavior?
3. How would this story change if it were told from Andre's point of view? How do you think he felt when Beauty first came to the castle?
4. Beauty returns the fallen bird to its nest even though she cynically thinks it will only fall again. In what ways is she like the bird? How do others in the story help lift her?
5. This story was originally titled *Beauty from Ash*, based on the conversation Beauty has with her father. How does Beauty wrestle good out of a terrible situation?
6. Roses and thorns play into the story in many ways. What were some of your favorite symbols or metaphors?
7. Beauty tries repeatedly to escape her trauma, including when

she's hoping to be eaten by the beast. In the end, how does she face her trauma? What gives her the courage to do so?

8. Early on, Beauty makes the joke that she and Beast should trade names. How do you think they each embody the ideas of "beauty" and "beast"?

If you have been a victim of sexual assault, you are not alone.
Please reach out.
National Sexual Assault Hotline
Available 24 hours a day
1-800-656-4673